LOST BRIDE

ALSO BY J.L. JARVIS

Drake & Wilde Mysteries
Love in the Time of Pumpkins
Secrets in the Hollow
Shadow of the Horseman

Standalones
A Kiss in the Rain
App-ily Ever After
Once Upon a Winter
The Red Rose
Highland Vow

Short Stories
Seasons of Love: A Short Story Collection
The Eleventh-Hour Pact
A Christmas Yarn
The Farmer and the Belle
Work-Crush Balance

Cedar Creek
Christmas at Cedar Creek
Snowstorm at Cedar Creek
Sunlight on Cedar Creek

Pine Harbor
Allison's Pine Harbor Summer
Evelyn's Pine Harbor Autumn

Lydia's Pine Harbor Christmas

Holiday House
The Christmas Cabin
The Winter Lodge
The Lighthouse
The Christmas Castle
The Beach House
The Christmas Tree Inn
The Holiday Hideaway

Highland Passage
Highland Passage
Knight Errant
Lost Bride

Highland Soldiers
The Enemy
The Betrayal
The Return
The Wanderer

American Hearts
Secret Hearts
Forbidden Hearts
Runaway Hearts

For more information, visit jljarvis.com.

Get monthly book news at news.jljarvis.com.

LOST BRIDE

A HIGHLAND PASSAGE NOVEL

J.L. JARVIS

LOST BRIDE
A Highland Passage Novel

Published by Bookbinder Press
bookbinderpress.com

ISBN (paperback) 978-1-942767-04-6
ISBN (hardcover) 978-1-942767-70-1
ISBN (ebook) 978-1-942767-03-9

CHAPTER 1

BEST LAID PLANS OF BRIDES AND MEN

The guests were all seated on white cloth-covered folding chairs with large bows on the back, and the weather was just as she'd dreamed it would be, with the morning sun shining as it should for a wedding. Lucy Buchanan lifted her face to the cool breeze as she looked at the sweeping carpet of green that sloped down to the sparkling Hudson River. It was time.

A stab of panic struck without warning. What had she done? This would be a life sentence. But she'd accepted it, and it was too late to turn back. Pulse racing, she took a deep breath, forced a smile, and pressed on down the aisle toward the altar. Everyone turned on the musical cue. With all eyes on the bride, the guests must have missed seeing the groom murmur something to the minister before he walked over to the pianist and cellist. They stopped playing. The groom picked up a microphone and turned to the guests.

Now several feet down the carpeted aisle, Lucy stopped. This was not what they'd rehearsed.

He cleared his throat. "Family and friends, I... uh... thank you for coming. I'm sorry, but there's not going to be a wedding today."

For Lucy, time stopped as a collective gasp was followed by heads turning en masse toward her. She could not move. Then the hushed murmurs crescendoed and rang in her ears. It was as if the wedding guests were all watching a tennis match as they looked from bride to groom then to bride. Tyler's eyes met Lucy's once before he turned and walked away. Lucy stood there, unable to move or react.

What happened next was a blur. People began to approach her. God bless them, her bridesmaids would not stop chattering well-meaning expressions of shock, sorrow, and support that were simply not helpful. On a day on which she was supposed to be the center of attention, she wanted to hide from the world. How could this have happened? Why her? She needed to think—or not think. Whichever it was, she desperately needed to do it alone.

Her mother-in-law—scratch that—her *would-have-been* mother-in-law was approaching. With lightning-fast reflexes, Lucy averted her eyes and pretended not to see the woman then fled in the other direction. Wearing the gown that had cost several paychecks, she fled into the woods in a billowing blur of white silk, leaving a trail of snagged shreds of lace and organza in her wake that would have made Hansel and Gretel proud. Voices called out, so she kept running in hope of escaping. Her heel caught on a tree root, and she fell. She looked up to find a man-made cave constructed of stacked rocks and dirt, with a few weeds and roots that had worked their way through.

She had seen one of these before. Putnam County, New York, was riddled with the mysterious stone chambers. They were a well-known local curiosity, but there was no definitive explanation for their presence. Theories abounded, ranging from extraterrestrial way stations to Neolithic structures built by the Celts. Lucy had settled upon the most logical—that they were the remains of early settlers' root cellars. After all, this was the land where the last of the Mohicans had roamed. Even today, parts of it looked as though nothing had changed in the past few hundred years—except people, evidently. Take Tyler Van Beek, her fiancé who had just left her at the altar. Hawkeye would never have done that to Cora. He'd jumped off a waterfall, for Pete's sake. Tyler Van Beek, on the other hand, had just jumped off a six-inch altar platform. Not quite the same thing.

Too angry for words, Lucy cursed Tyler as she pounded the earth that covered the chamber. "Ow!" Apparently, there was a little more rock than earth. Once more, she cursed, this time from the pain. But a light came from inside the chamber. "It must be my burning rage," she muttered to herself.

A voice called out from behind her.

"Oh no." They were coming for her in a fluttering mass of moss-green bridesmaids' gowns. Lucy ducked into the chamber. Her dress caught on something. The tearing sound that came next made her wince, but then she reminded herself that she would never be wearing that dress again. Ever. Inside the stone chamber, she walked toward the light. Walking toward the light in a tunnel might not have been a good sign of things to come, but it was that or face the bridesmaids. She would not have it get back to Tyler that tears had been shed. One of her friends would let something slip. And that person would tell someone else, until it got back to that jilting, spineless, exoskeletal, cold-footed coward! God, she loved him.

She emerged from the tunnel feeling very empowered after having wiped dry the evidence of the ugly blubbering that may have occurred in the chamber. So much for walking toward the light. That was gone. A thick fog had rolled in. After taking a couple of steps, she stopped, afraid she might fall into the Hudson.

To test the visibility in true storm-chaser style, she stretched out her arm. Nope. She couldn't see her hand. She could feel it was wet, though. A light, drizzling rain was beginning to fall.

Pounding hooves shook the spongy ground. That didn't seem right. Then a curse cut through the sound of the rain. She looked up to see a horse and rider break through the mist. A strong arm hooked around her waist from behind and yanked her back just as a horse reared up and galloped past. She and her strong-armed rescuer fell to the ground. She looked up into the deep-set eyes of the man lying on top of her. For a moment, she lay there, stunned by the fall or transfixed by his gaze. She couldn't have said which at the moment. Rain drizzled down both their faces.

"Are you all right?" he asked, his brown eyes filled with concern.

"Yes, I think so." Her eyes drifted down to his lips—not because she found them attractive, per se, but because they were mere inches from hers. Of course, from a purely objective standpoint, one could say they fell within the realm of attractive. In addition, from that same purely objective standpoint, she was losing her mind. What sane person would just lie there? Her eyes darted to the hand on her shoulder. It was large. He immediately removed it and got up. With a firm grasp, he took hold of her hand and pulled her to her feet.

His mood instantly changed. "Are you daft? What do you think you're doing out here in the rain?" Without waiting for an answer, he grasped her hand as though she were a child and guided her along behind him. To where, she had no idea.

Disoriented, Lucy looked about at her surroundings. "It wasn't raining a minute ago."

He frowned. "It's been raining all day." When his stare had completely unsettled her, his eyes drifted down to her silk-and-organza gown, now muddy and limp.

"Are you sure you're all right?"

Her head felt fuzzy and tingly, and this guy sounded like Sean Connery. But why would Sean Connery be rescuing her from galloping horses? Come to think of it, why were there galloping horses to be rescued from? She had to be dreaming. Or maybe she'd injured her head in that fall.

"Lassie?"

"Lucy." It was a reflexive response. She'd thought he had called her by name. By the time she realized her mistake, she'd already spoken. Now he knew one more thing about her than she knew about him. Not that she wanted to know much about him, except who he was and where they were going.

"*Lucy*." Her name sounded better when he said it. Too bad her name wasn't longer. And then there was the touch of his hand as he held hers and the way he studied her until she blushed, which was no small feat, given the day she'd had. Which reminded her, what the heck was going on?

"I'm Rory."

That wasn't exactly what she'd been wondering, but hey, good to know. "Rory." She eyed his kilt. "More like Rob Rory." She chuckled, alone. "Sorry, it's a thing I do —make lame jokes under stress. It's a coping mechanism I can't seem to control." She winced then extended her hand. "Good to meet you. I'm Lucy Buchanan—almost Van Beek, but not really. So where are we?"

He took in the landscape with a sweeping glance. "Everything you see here is Munro land."

"Oh," she said, still confused. "Munro land. So... kind of like Disneyland but without all the rides?"

"Disney? I've not heard of that clan."

Lucy smiled. She was actually smiling despite everything—well, despite just the one thing really, but it was a biggie. She looked down the dirt road. "So who was that insane bastard on the horse?"

"Ah, that insane bastard was my brother."

"Oh. Sorry."

"No need to apologize. You're a fine judge of character—although he's not actually a bastard. He's quite legitimate, and in line to inherit a fortune. I'm the second son, and I'm not."

"A bastard or in line to inherit a fortune?"

He started to answer, but she said, "I was kidding." She began laughing a little too hard then caught herself before the tears started.

He tilted his head and peered at her. "Lass?"

What seemed to capture his interest was a mystery to

her. He must have picked up on her subtle internal hysteria.

"Yes, lad?" Stress made her snarky. She winced as she brushed herself off, only managing to smear dirt on her bodice and skirt. It was hopeless. She looked as if she'd been dragged through the mud, and her wrist hurt along with her backside and elbow. "I'm sorry. Do I know you? Were you at the wedding? I'm sorry the show was canceled."

"The show?" He peered at her as though she had just come unhinged.

She shook her head. "Never mind. I was just being funny. Or not. Being left at the altar does that to me. Just hilarious." She felt herself starting to cry, which was not going to happen. Not now. Not for that numbnuts Tyler the Timid-hearted. She steeled herself and looked at the man before her. Not too shabby once she got past the distractingly muscular shoulders and chest. Then there was his face. A girl could get a stiff neck looking up at that face and not mind it. Not that he was perfect. He wasn't. He was more rugged than handsome, with large facial features and straight chestnut hair tousled as though he didn't care how it looked. And why would he need to? It looked great from where she was standing. Yeah, this guy was the type she had always avoided—the dangerous kind. "So, uh..."

"May I?" He leaned closer and pointed at her forehead, which apparently had something on it.

She swiped the back of her hand across her forehead then shrugged as though it were futile. "I looked so pretty this morning with my airbrushed makeup and a fresh mani-pedi. That was before my groom left me at the altar and walked away with my hopes and dreams. Then I dragged my beautiful dress through the woods, pretty much did a face-plant into—man, I hope that was dirt—and then I was knocked to the ground, as you know, and for which I am very thankful, by the way. But still, at this point, does a smudge on my face really matter?"

His eyes softened as he gazed at her. "I think you look bonnie."

She took in a breath. "Oh, wow! Would you mind just stopping by every morning and saying that to me? And then maybe again during my afternoon slump at work—about 2:15, 2:30..."

He gazed back in silence.

"I'm just kidding, of course. I mean, that would be crazy. You could just make a GIF." She made a goofy face.

"Make a what?"

"You know, a video on a loop..." She spoke in a throaty, low pitch and attempted his accent. "'I think you look bonnie. I think you look bonnie. I think you look bonnie.'" She burst into laughter.

He gave her a blank stare.

She averted her eyes. "Yeah. Never mind." She glanced about, uneasy because he was still watching her.

A droplet fell from her hair to her nose, and he wiped it off with his finger as he gazed into her eyes. Then he took the end of his plaid and squeezed it about her dripping, shoulder-length hair. She was too startled and cold to resist.

That might have been a good time to wake up before she swooned—not that she was one prone to swooning, but it was a dream, after all. On the other hand, what safer place was there to swoon than a dream? She'd already been horizontal, so why not? *And, c'mon, look at this guy!* When he looked at her, she knew she'd been looked at. And those arms—sturdy without being steroidal.

"What were you doing out there on the road in the mist? My bastard brother might have trampled your bonnie behind."

Bonnie behind? Well, that was a little personal. She wasn't sure whether to thank him or smack him. She frowned. His Scottish accent was thick. Otherwise, she might have understood him quickly enough to respond with something more than her current slack jaw.

"I don't see many Scotsmen on horseback, so you caught me off guard." She looked down and did a double take as she spied his hand on the hilt of a sword. Suddenly, her bonnie behind was the least of her concerns. While his hand merely rested upon his sword at the moment, in an instant, he might whisk that sword out of its scabbard and point it at her. With a smile that didn't come close to looking as casual as she'd intended, she took a step back. "Anyway, enjoyed the chat. Gotta go!" She turned and began to march off.

He grabbed her wrist. "Where do you think you're going?"

She did her best to behave as if she were not terrified that he might swing his sword in her general direction. "I don't know. I thought I might go back to my car and drive home."

"Lucy, I can hardly allow you to wander off to your peril."

"That's awfully nice, but—"

"There's an inn over there." He nodded back in the

direction the horse had come from. Through the mist, she could faintly make out a stone-walled structure.

"Oh, an inn, huh?" He didn't waste any time. "No, thanks. I'll just go back where I came from."

His smile faded a bit as he studied her closely. "Back where? There's nothing back there."

"You're wrong."

"I daresay I'm not. I've lived here all my life."

"And I've lived back there part of mine. So if you don't mind, I'll be on my way."

"To where? Do you even ken where you are?"

Well, okay, she would play along—but only one round just to humor him. She looked beyond to a dirt road that sloped upward through waving grasses to the green hills beyond. There were very few trees, which made the hills appear clad in soft blankets of deep green. She'd never seen anything like it—except—ah, yes. She'd only been once, during a backpacking summer in her college days. But those few days had left an impression. "Wild guess, Scotland?"

"Aye."

Of course it was Scotland. And that was how she knew she was dreaming. She loved Scotland, which was why she and Tyler had chosen it for their honeymoon. Well, there it was. That explained everything. Along with the wedding, their honeymoon in Scotland had been on her mind, so she was dreaming about it. Good, that was settled. Except why was she dreaming of Scotland with some brawny dude? *Don't overthink it. You'll be awake soon.*

Dark clouds blew in as Lucy and her Scottish mystery man took a few steps. Lightning cut through the sky and lit up the stone structure she'd just come from. To Lucy, it looked like a rounded pile of stones, only hollow. She walked toward it. Light shone through the doorway. They both stepped closer and looked inside. Lucy saw straight through to the woods she had come from. A gaggle of moss-green-clad bridesmaids and a couple of groomsmen stared back at her. Her mother made her way through the middle of them and stopped, appearing stunned. They all stood there, like a portrait of pitying looks.

Without taking his eyes from them, Rory asked, "Who are those creatures?"

"My bridesmaids. And that one in the middle is my mom." Lucy called through the chamber, "It's okay, Mom. I'm fine."

"Och, they're people? Dressed as they are in the color of fairies, I thought..."

Tyler made his way to the front of the group and called out to her. Their eyes met.

Lucy muttered to herself, "You're dead to me, Tyler. Go away."

Then lightning struck just a few feet away and split a tree down the middle. Lucy flinched, and Rory held on to her shoulders with steadying hands.

Lucy looked up. "I didn't mean it."

When she turned back, the opening was gone. A wall of stones stood in its place. Lucy waited in hope that the wall would reopen. When she finally resigned herself to the fact that it was not going to open, she looked up at Rory, her mouth still agape.

"Could you use a wee dram?"

"Yes!" Maybe that sounded a bit too enthusiastic, but

at least she was honest. "What if my fiancé—or whatever he is now—comes looking for me?"

"Your what?"

"My fiancé. The man in that stone chamber. He might come looking for me."

"As he should. What sort of man would leave a bonnie lassie—or Lucy—out wandering alone?"

She gave those sparkling eyes her best withering stare. "I'm allowed out on my own now and then—if I'm good."

He lifted a brow and revealed even, white teeth through a cockeyed smile. "As I imagine you are."

That was it. She hauled off and punched him. Then cursed. The man's abs were rock solid, unlike her fist. Apparently, she was a vivid dreamer. Her knuckles still hurt from the impact.

He offered her his arm and tilted his head toward the inn. He frowned and waited for a while. Then he shook his head and wrapped the end of his plaid about her head and shoulders. "We'll go inside and wait for your fancy man."

"Fiancé," she said as they walked toward the inn. "It might be a while."

"Lovers' tiff, was it?"

"No. Not exactly. And don't look so amused."

He tossed her a curious glance as he opened the heavy oak door to the inn.

CHAPTER 2
TAKING WHISKY
FROM A STRANGER

I nside, the inn smelled of baking bread, ale, and smoke from the fire. A man staggered past them to the stairs. *Whew!* Someone didn't get the memo about antiperspirant. Still, the place was sheltered and dry, so she couldn't complain. Everyone wore the same sort of costume, as if they were part of a Renaissance fair. One man, looking the worse for wear, lay draped over a table, asleep and contentedly snoring, his hand still grasping a pewter flagon of ale.

Lucy didn't know what to make of the place. It had to be one of those historic pubs with the old, dark wood paneling and benches they all had. She'd visited more than a few of those pubs during her carefree college backpacking days, and they all had a similar look, especially after a couple of beers. But the clientele hadn't dressed quite like these people. No, if she wasn't drunk, then she had to be dreaming.

Rory led her to a blazing peat fire, where he set a chair down before her and gestured for her to sit. "Dry yourself here by the fire." Without asking, he unfastened her hair clip and unpinned her soggy bridal updo.

"Oh!" Startled, she began to protest. "Well..." She was not nearly as comfortable with his hands on her as he was. It wasn't that the touching was so wrong. After all, it was only her hair. "Well, okay."

But it didn't feel okay. It felt way better than that, which was when she began to feel guilty. Until a few hours ago, the only hands in her hair—not counting her stylist's—had been Tyler's, and not all that often. She quietly breathed in through her nose just to make sure she wouldn't sigh as he combed his fingers through her hair by the heat of the fire.

He stopped, and she missed him already.

"Wait here. I'll get us something to drink."

Lucy looked into the fire and tried to make sense of her day, which she should've conceded was not going to happen.

"A FALL WEDDING WOULD BE PERFECT!" How well she remembered that moment not one year ago. She'd said yes. How could she not have? And they had celebrated— well, they'd gone to tell Tyler's parents. They had proceeded to spend the whole evening in his parents' Westchester mansion, backs straight, hands folded, and knees pressed together. They'd all agreed it was a perfect match.

Her life had always seemed perfect in everyone else's eyes. She had sailed through school to college and grad-uate school, lined up a job before graduation, and met

Tyler in a training seminar during her first week on the job. They'd been together for nearly five years before Tyler popped the question. Well, if glancing up over his laptop to posit—in the same tone of voice he used when making a tee time—his reasoning as to why marriage would be a logical step at this point in their lives could be considered a proposal, then yes, he had proposed.

He'd startled her, really. They had both been buried in work, he with a computer programming crisis, and she with a sales team communication challenge.

"Okay. Let's talk about it after we come up for air." And she looked back down at her laptop and returned to her usual work-stress balance. She'd always assumed a formal question-popping would follow at some point after his impromptu presentation. It hadn't. But no worries, that was just Tyler's way. He was good and kind and everything a future husband should be. And he loved her. She paused to ponder. She was pretty sure he loved her. Who would spend seven years with someone they didn't love? Of course he loved her. They were destined to be happy. After all, it wasn't as though there were any scary mysteries ahead. They'd lived together, kicked the tires, and perfected the fit, end of story. They were going to be married and live happily ever after. Happily. Ever. After.

WHICH WAS why she was lost God knew where in a setting that made no more sense than the rest of her life at the moment. A chilly breeze found its way in through the cracks in the windows and doors, catching the flames in the nearby fireplace. She glanced over at Rory, who was engaged in a chat with the innkeeper. And there Lucy was... how or why, she had no idea. All she knew was that her stomach felt as if she were riding the waves of the raging North Sea.

She shivered. Rory appeared with a crumpled tartan he'd apparently borrowed. He arranged it over her shoulders and sat down beside her with one arm protectively draped over the back of her chair.

He offered her a glass of amber liquid. "Here, drink this."

Lucy drank it straight down. "Oh, this is good. What is it?"

He eyed her as though he did not quite believe her. "Lass, have you never had whisky?"

"I'm more of a wine drinker, myself. But that felt so warm going down. May I have another?"

With a crooked smile, Rory nodded and went to the bar. This time, he returned with a bottle, which Lucy generously poured into her glass and proceeded to drink.

"Easy."

She gave him a cross look. "It's not like I haven't had alcohol before. I've been to college."

Rory leaned back and folded his arms. "It's a wee bit stronger than wine."

The plaid slipped off Lucy's shoulder, so Rory wrapped it around her again. Whether he'd pressed her head to his sturdy shoulder or she had collapsed from exhaustion, she wasn't quite sure. She thought about lifting her head to sit up on her own, but the truth was, his shoulder felt warm. With a sudden longing for that same warmth to surround her, she turned her face to his shoulder and breathed in. Wild grass and fresh sweat—he smelled manly. Wow, was this dream ever vivid.

"Are you sniffing me, lass?" Small lines formed at the outside corners of his eyes when he smiled.

"No!" She came to her senses and assumed a shocked expression.

His crooked smile told her he wasn't buying any of it. On the other hand, he didn't seem to mind, either. She couldn't help but be charmed—because she was human, and who wouldn't be? They didn't make men like him anymore. He was all man and knew it. She lifted her chin and looked away even though she could still feel his eyes on her. Could the guy ever stare! In a good way—not a creepy one. He watched her as though he wanted to protect her, which was new and felt good... too good. That was bad. It was way too soon. She was simply reacting to what Tyler had done by pretending he hadn't hurt her.

But if she had to have a rebound man, why not have one who was thoughtful, strong, and good looking? Wow, the fire was warm.

"Was that him I saw?"

"Who?"

"Your fiancé man."

"A simple 'fiancé' will do," she corrected.

Rory looked at her with feigned pity. "Oh, he's simple, is he?"

"No." Was he deliberately trying to irk her? From his smug expression, she was sure that answer was yes.

"Was that him in the cairn?"

"In the what?"

"In the rocks?"

"Oh." Her lip curled as she recalled seeing Tyler. So he'd seen it too. She thought maybe she'd been hallucinating. Could one even hallucinate while dreaming? Wouldn't that be kind of redundant? *Whatever.*

Rory settled comfortably back in his chair. "They call it the fairy cairn."

Well, wasn't he the informative Scottish tour guide? With nothing better to do at the moment, she played along. "Why?"

"It's said strange things happen there, as you and I have both seen."

She ignored his knowing look. "That's just one of those stories—like the Loch Ness Monster—to boost tourism."

He watched her with narrowing eyes. "We both know that's not true."

"The Loch Ness Monster?"

"The fairy cairn."

When she could stand it no more, she turned her gaze from the fire to him. "Things like that don't just happen."

He regarded her as though she should know as well as he did what the truth was. And the worst part was that she did. "We both saw him," Rory said after a long pause.

She finally gave up resisting and reluctantly nodded. "I'm not dreaming, am I?"

He shook his head then leaned forward and propped his elbows on his knees. "When I was a wee lad, I was warned not to go near the cairn or the fairies would take me. All the children were told the same thing. But I wanted to see for myself. So one day, while my father had stopped for a wee dram at the inn, I snuck outside for a look. It was hollow and perfect to play in, so in I went.

From the outside, it had only one entrance. But inside, I discovered another opening. My good sense told me to go back, but I ignored it. I saw things on the other side that I'd never seen before or since. An iron giant came at me and nearly killed me. I ran back to the cairn, terrified out of my wits. I told my older brother, Angus, what had happened. He laughed, of course, so I never spoke of it again, until now." He leveled a piercing gaze into her eyes. "But you understand, for you've been through the cairn."

For a moment, she was unable to speak. She shook her head slowly. "It's a root cellar. They're all over Putnam County and parts of New England. You can't always see them for the trees and the weeds, but they're there. Anyway, when Tyler—well, never mind that—I just needed a moment. And there was a light from the other side, so I was only going to hide 'til they all went away. It sounds so ridiculous now." She stared straight ahead for a long while then whispered, "This can't be happening. It must be the stress from the wedding—or rather, the non-wedding." She took in a sharp breath. "What year is it now?" She lifted her eyes, afraid of the answer.

"It's 1746."

Lucy shut her eyes while the numbers sank in. Fear mixed with confusion as she looked into his eyes. "That's two hundred and I can't even count how many years ago."

"I'm sorry."

The more sympathetic he sounded, the worse Lucy felt. "My head hurts." She buried her face in her hands for a moment then took in a breath and sat up. "I don't know what to do. I mean, going home would be nice. But the opening closed up. I watched it." Her speech had grown faster with each frantic thought.

"We'll figure it out."

"Will we?"

He nodded as though he was sure. "Aye."

She liked how that sounded. "But... how?"

"We'll put one foot in front of the other until we end up somewhere."

Lucy lifted an eyebrow. "And to think, people spend money on life coaches."

A moment's confusion passed over his face. "Aye, well, the first step is to head for home before the rain starts again."

"Home?" She could only imagine where that might be. But where didn't actually matter, since she was not in the habit of riding off with perfect strangers—although in this case, he *was* actually perfect.

"'Tis not far."

"Thank you, but I can't go home with you."

With a nod, he said, "I ken you're afraid, but you need not be. I'll keep you safe. I give you my word."

His word. When was the last time anyone's word was his bond? People shook hands all the time. It meant nothing. And yet, oddly, she trusted this man. He had a gentle manner, the sort only a tall, strapping man could afford to reveal. He seemed trustworthy. But newspaper archives were full of stories about young, innocent women who went off with seemingly trustworthy men. And they never came back.

Seeing her hesitation, Rory said, "I cannae just leave you here—alone with this lot."

She looked about at the handful of tavern patrons, most of whom were currently sleeping it off from the previous night. "They seem harmless enough, except that one over there staring at me. He looks like kind of a jerk."

He raised his eyebrows with a questioning look.

She thought for a moment. "A rogue... or a scoundrel."

He tilted his head and considered. "A jerk."

With a nod, Lucy said, "He's probably harmless."

Rory looked doubtful.

Lucy considered her options. It wasn't as though there were many options, just the two—stay or go. She supposed the man she was with was better than the soused, smelly lot there in the inn. And so far, Rory had behaved like a perfect gentleman. Why did the word "perfect" work its way into her every thought about him? She needed to decide. Her immediate future hung in the balance, and neither choice was ideal. But she looked about. Based on smell alone, this man won, hands down. And he did have some manners. Still unsure, she had to say something. "Okay."

Before she could have second thoughts, they both emptied their glasses. Lucy reached for the bottle, but Rory gently took it from her and set it down on the table as the two of them headed outside to his horse. Rory swung himself up in one motion then held out his hand.

"But—"

With one strong motion, he pulled her up behind him. "Hold on." When she failed to do so, he reached back and brought both her arms about his waist. "Ready?"

"No." She wasn't kidding.

And with that, they rode off.

"Won't it look improper for you to be bringing a strange woman home?" Lucy had read a few Jane Austen novels. She knew how it was. People would talk. She and Rory would be shunned by the town. She supposed she could weather that storm, but could he? And yet, as she clung to his waist, her body pressed against his, she became more concerned about his prospects of being alone with her. She was reluctant to admit it, even to herself, but there was something about him that thrilled her—no, troubled her. That was what she meant. For starters, his touch was electric, and his straight brown hair touched his thick neck and collar in just the right way. Lucy shook her head. This was only a reaction to being dumped at the altar. She was already vulnerable, and now she was lost. Latching on to a good-looking man was a great way to avoid facing her problems alone. That was all it was. Her wild attraction to Rory would fade, and she would wonder what she'd ever seen in this guy with his coarse shock of hair and broad shoulders—not to mention his dark eyebrows and deep-set brown eyes that she could drown in. Nope. Nothing to look at there.

At some point during her musings, the skies opened up and began pelting them with rain as they pressed on toward Rory's home. They rode through a glen to the foot of a hill that he'd called a brae, where a large building loomed. "Don't tell me you live there."

"All right."

"I mean... wow. And you're sure that the, uh, lord of the castle won't mind if I visit?"

"He'll likely not know. My father's been ill and confined to his bed."

Rory left his horse with a boy in the stable and led her inside, where they stood by the warmth of the fire. No one was about at the late hour. Feeling his eyes upon her, Lucy glanced around the room—everywhere except at him.

"Do I make you nervous?"

She averted her eyes. "Of course not." *I am such a liar.*

"You're safe here." He took a step toward her and lifted her hands in his. "I promise."

"It's not you." Well, that wasn't quite true. "It's all just a lot to take in."

"And you must be exhausted. Wait here while I arrange for someone to prepare your bedchamber."

Lucy surveyed the room lit by flickering firelight. The ceilings were tall, with large paintings and tapestries hanging about. Even in the dim light, it looked sumptuous. If she had to get lost in the past, she may as well have wound up with a good-looking guy in a castle. All things considered, she'd done well.

Rory returned with a housemaid in tow as he gave her instructions. "Effie, would you show Miss..."

"Buchanan."

"Miss Buchanan to her room. Oh, and find her something to wear."

"Sir?"

Rory paused in his tracks and thought for a moment. "Give her one of Mistress Munro's gowns."

Mistress Munro. Lucy took note. Mother? Sister-in-law? Maybe wife?

Effie's eyes widened, but a stern look from Rory sent her eyes downward.

Turning to Lucy, he said, "Should you need anything, you have only to ask Effie here."

"Come, Miss Buchanan," Effie said.

With reluctance, Lucy thanked him and left.

CHAPTER 3
A CASTLE OF GHOSTS

Now properly dressed, she descended the wide stairway. No one was about except for a house-maid who was busily dusting. Lucy walked along a long corridor lined with antlers until she came to an open door. Thick carpet lay on the floor, and the walls were practically covered in paintings, most of them portraits. It was not unlike the castles she'd toured, except furniture and other items that ought to be old were quite new. A man in a kilt seemed to look down at her from across the room. She drew closer and studied the painting. He looked awfully stern. She moved on to the next. The man in that portrait was younger, and not all that bad looking for a dude in a portrait.

"He was my grandfather." How long Rory had been standing there, watching, she couldn't begin to guess.

"He looks nice." What else could she say? He didn't look half as sour as the pruney guy next to him.

Rory's mouth twitched with a hint of a grin. "He had his moments."

Lucy's eyes wandered along to the next portrait. That man looked like Rory, although not quite as broad in the shoulders, and with lighter chestnut-colored hair. Lucy looked from the painting to Rory, comparing.

"My father. He was about my age when that was painted. He's rather ill at the moment, but when he's feeling better, I'll introduce you."

"I'll look forward to that."

"As should he."

She glanced down as if his admiring smile were like the sun, too much to take in directly. Color tinted her cheeks. Wow, she was easy—and foolish. He was just being a charming host. And there she was, acting as though he'd just asked her to the junior prom. She took a step toward the next portrait. The sooner she moved the discussion forward, the less likely he would be to notice her schoolgirl blush. She looked up at a young woman in a simple and elegant gown. "She's very beautiful."

His eyes darkened as he looked at the portrait.

"Who is she?" When he failed to answer, Lucy turned from the portrait.

Rory's jaw tightened but just as quickly relaxed. "Margery."

"Another Munro?" Lucy asked as she continued to admire the portrait. "And she is..."

"My wife."

Lucy's jaw dropped. There was something about the way he had said it that gave her a chill. "Oh. I didn't know you were married."

"*Was* married. She's dead," he said bluntly.

"I'm so sorry."

He met her eyes to acknowledge the thought then

looked quickly away. "I think dinner must be ready." He turned and walked with such long strides that he left Lucy trailing behind. So dinner was lunch, she surmised while she walked, and someone had mood swings. She found herself in a dining room as she'd expected. What she didn't expect was that they would be alone. "Won't your brother be joining us?"

"I doubt it. I imagine he's sleeping off last night's whisky. I'm sorry if my bluntness disturbs you."

"It doesn't." What she left out was that Rory's gruff manner did.

Rory continued. "My—what was it you called him?— oh yes, my bastard of a brother tends to do most of his sleeping by daylight."

"So he's part vampire, is he?"

With a grimace, he dismissed the topic.

"I was kidding." Apparently humor wasn't his thing.

A brusque nod and awkward silence followed, broken only by the scurry of servants about them, serving their meal.

Lucy was lifting a spoonful of soup to her lips when the door opened. A man of about Rory's age stood in the doorway and stared straight at Lucy. He had the same hair color but with more waves, and his features were finer.

"Mr. Angus Munro, allow me to introduce Miss Lucy Buchanan."

Angus lowered his chin and smiled slyly. "It's an honor to meet you, Miss Buchanan." He eyed Rory with a raised eyebrow. "Margery's dress fits her well."

Rory's eyes flashed as Angus swaggered to his seat. When he was settled, Rory said, "Miss Buchanan is my honored guest. I expect her to be treated as such."

Angus's mouth twitched, half smiling. "Would I do otherwise?"

Rory's eyes narrowed, which seemed to amuse Angus. He settled his gaze upon Lucy. "How is it I've never had the pleasure of meeting the charming Miss Lucy Buchanan?"

"I've just arrived." She stopped short when Rory flashed her a look of warning.

"Miss Buchanan is a distant cousin by marriage," Rory said. "I willnae bore you with the details."

"Thank you for that," Angus drawled then took a drink of wine. When he set his glass down, he lifted his eyes to meet Lucy's.

There was no denying his charm, but it appeared too well practiced from Lucy's perspective. Perhaps that was due to his assessing eye, which made her uneasy. She glanced down at her dress—Margery's dress. Looking up at Rory, she asked, "How long were you married?"

Angus leaned back in his chair and observed their interaction with a glint in his eyes. Setting down his soup-spoon with a clink, Rory stood and dropped his napkin to his chair. "I'm afraid I've lost my appetite. If you'll excuse me."

If clearly wasn't an option since he was already halfway to the door.

"I'm so sorry," Lucy said. "I shouldn't have said anything."

"Och! They were only married a few months. He's had five years to get over it." Angus resumed eating.

"Only a few months? How sad." She couldn't imagine what it would be like to get married and lose your true love so quickly. Of course, she hadn't married at all before losing hers, but Rory had lost his to death. Lucy wouldn't wish that even on Tyler.

A faraway look passed over Angus's face, but his eyes brightened as he turned back to Lucy. "He needs to get on with his life, but he refuses to let go of the past."

"He must have loved her very much."

With a nod, Angus said, "She was a beauty."

"I feel terrible for upsetting him."

"Oh, I wouldnae worry about Rory."

But she did. She couldn't help but be curious about Margery's death, but she'd done enough damage to dare say any more. Still, she wondered. How young she must have been. And what a tragedy when modern medicine probably held the cure. But these were not modern times. Rory was an uncommon man, whose love was deep and everlasting. He had clearly been devastated by his wife's death, and Lucy had opened the wound.

Mercifully, the next course arrived, and her conversation with Angus moved on.

Lucy spent the rest of the afternoon on her own. After choosing a book from the library, she went to her room and sat down to read. With a sigh, she gave up, too distracted to focus on her book. She could not stop thinking about what had happened at dinner. She supposed she'd known at the time that she was treading on dangerous ground, but her curiosity had gotten the better of her. Lesson learned. Rory Munro seemed to guard his privacy like Fort Knox. Why she had bothered to ask in the first place, she couldn't really say, except that she had been genuinely curious about him. There was no sensible reason for that. She was leaving tomorrow, so his personal life should have been left on a need-to-know basis. And yet, for the sake of her selfish curiosity, she'd asked him, effectively poking a stick at an unhealed wound. She vowed to proceed with more care in the future. After all, she was in a strange place with manners and customs and a host whom she could not decipher. Wasn't it enough that he'd welcomed her into his home? Otherwise, she would have wandered the Highlands alone. His life was his own. She had no business prying.

THERE WAS little daylight left by the time Effie knocked on the door and informed her that Mr. Rory Monroe would not be joining her for supper and Mr. Angus Munro had gone out. The housemaid then asked if she would care for a tray in her room. Lucy welcomed the chance to dine without having to worry what she might say or do next to offend her host.

A storm blew in, bringing wind that howled and rattled the window. Lucy finished her supper and read a few chapters of her book. Sometime later, she stood by the fire in a nightgown and robe, warming herself. A quiet knock sounded on her door.

She opened it to find Rory standing there, looking far more composed than the last time she'd seen him. "Are you comfortable, lass?"

"Yes, I am. You've been very kind."

"Anyone would have done the same."

"But you did, and I thank you."

He gave her a slight nod. "Tomorrow, I'll take you to the cairn." He lingered for a moment then turned to leave.

"Rory, I'm sorry about before. It was none of my business."

He shook his head to dismiss her concerns. With a warm smile, he bade her good night.

"Goodnight, Rory."

After the door had closed between them, she sat down by the fire and breathed in the pungent aroma of peat. Tomorrow, she would be home.

RORY RETURNED TO HIS ROOM, poured a whisky, and sank into a chair by the fire. He had neglected to tell Lucy how many times he had gone to the cairn and tried to find a way back in time so he could fix what had gone wrong in his own life. He had come to accept that, for him, it was not meant to be. Tomorrow, she would expect to walk through the cairn and go back to her life as though nothing had happened. For her sake, he hoped she would fare better than he had.

He'd been stuck for so long in his purgatory on earth that he'd long ago given up hope of escaping his fate. He'd even gone off to war with the Black Watch and fought in Flanders, but not out of bravery. On the contrary, he'd lacked the courage to take his own life, so he had hoped someone else might do it for him. Somewhere along the way, he'd gotten used to existing. As long as his days had routine and purpose, he managed to get through them, one by one. He was hailed as a fearless member of the Black Watch, who'd run headlong into danger without flinching. Little did anyone know that the thing he feared most was his future, for he was destined to spend it alone.

He let out a derisive laugh at the thought of his future, of fate, and of time itself. Everyone always thought they had time to build the life they sought. But time was a myth meant to assuage people. He took another drink.

Why did he persist in going around and around the same thoughts, only to wind up in the same place? At least, for the moment, he had someone to think about other than himself. In truth, he liked Lucy, and he worried about her. He wouldn't wish his family on anyone, but there was a good chance she would be forced to remain and become part of the household. She was better off here than out wandering the Highlands alone—but not much.

He admired how she'd managed so far. She hadn't sniveled or whined. Had she done so, he would have dropped her off up in the hills and left her to wander the wild Highlands alone. Then he smiled to himself. No, he never would have done that. His heart may have grown cold, but it had not grown as hard as all that. In truth, he felt a softness toward Miss Lucy Buchanan. The lass touched him in a way he hadn't felt since Margery. He swallowed down an unwelcome surge of emotion. The feelings came back even now in odd moments when he didn't expect them. Love was like that. And that was why he could not let himself love again.

That was Angus's duty. As the oldest, it fell to him to marry and produce an heir, although he'd shown no signs of fulfilling that duty. Given Rory's past dealings with fate, he could fully envision going through all the trouble of marrying without love simply to produce an heir in Angus's stead, only for Angus to suddenly marry and have his own son, leaving Rory to suffer with a wife he didn't love. He wouldn't put it past Angus to do such a thing solely for his own amusement. So no, that was one responsibility Rory would not take on in Angus's behalf.

Plumes of smoke drifted up from the fire. Rory watched them, transfixed, and slowly exhaled. His father lay sick, and his rake of a brother was busy with his own self-indulgent pursuits. So it had fallen to Rory to manage the estate and perform all the duties his brother neglected. He couldn't remember when that hadn't been the case. Even when they were young, the less Angus had done, the more he had been adored. When his mother was alive, she would often pull Rory aside and gently try to explain the unexplainable: why Rory could not please his father enough. His mother had all but made up for it with her warmth and her devotion. Then the cholera had come and taken her from him. From age ten, all he had left to take with him through life was the memory from his mother of what love could be and the reminder from his father of what it was not. Someday his father would die, never knowing in what little regard his beloved first son had held him. And Rory's regard—Rory's love—would mean nothing.

So that was the existence to which Rory was destined, to live in a castle of ghosts and misplaced affection. Surrounded by specters of love and belonging, Rory persevered with a deeply ingrained sense of duty he could not seem to shake. But in the midst of it all, he was alone.

CHAPTER 4
ROAD CLOSED

Once more, Lucy emerged from the cairn, forcing back desperate longing for something that just couldn't be.

"I'm sorry, lass."

She lifted her chin and looked bravely at him. "Well, I'll just have to keep trying."

He smiled and gave her an encouraging nod. "Aye, that you will."

"In the meanwhile, I need a job."

"Are you daft?"

"I don't think so, although I do seem to be suffering under the impression that I've traveled through time to 1746—not exactly the bellwether of a person who's sane. But I'll earn my keep." Although, as she said it, she wasn't quite sure how. She couldn't imagine there was much of a demand in 1746 for a marketing representative.

"You're a guest in my home. I'll not have you insulting my hospitality by working. It would reflect badly on me, and you wouldnae want that."

He almost appeared to be smiling, but she couldn't be sure. There were times when she wasn't quite sure how to take Rory. And after the previous night, she wasn't taking any chances.

They rode home in comfortable silence. As they drew close to the castle, Lucy asked, "Would you mind if I walked the rest of the way?"

He pulled on the reins to bring his horse to a stop. "Would you mind if I joined you?"

That surprised her. "No, not at all." She hadn't expected him to spend any more time with her than he had to, but there they were, walking. She considered her words with great care before speaking. "About last night..."

He shook his head to dismiss her, but she pressed on. "I'm sorry. It was none of my business. I suppose I could say I was just trying to make conversation, but I was genuinely interested."

He cast a sharp eye in her direction but then looked straight ahead. "Dinnae waste your interest on me—or your time."

"Well, at the moment, time seems to be all that I have."

"I've got nothing of interest to benefit you or anyone else." He resumed walking.

"I wasn't asking for anything. I just meant you're an interesting person, and frankly, I could use a friend here."

He appeared a little insulted. "Have I not made you feel welcome?"

"Yes, of course. I just meant—look, sorry I asked. Never mind." She was growing a little frustrated for being made to feel guilty for making conversation. She could only imagine this guy at a water cooler. He would be the life of the cube dwellers. But he was her host, so she would try to overlook his irritable manner. "I'm sorry. I know you've been hurt. Angus told me—"

Rory stopped and turned to face her, his eyes bright with anger. "What did he tell you?"

She was taken aback by what seemed like an overreaction. "Well, he told me you'd only been married a few months before Margery died."

Rory let out a bitter laugh. "Oh, did he?"

Lucy nodded, confused.

"And that's all he told you?"

"Yes." If she didn't know better, she would have thought he was amused.

Rory resumed walking. "You were right. He really is a bastard."

She took quick steps to keep up. "Rory—"

With a bitter smile, he said, "Enough about me. Let's talk about things that are painful to you, like your wedding."

Lucy stopped. She felt as if she'd been punched in the gut. "I guess I had that coming," she said softly.

Rory's brow furrowed, perhaps with regret, but he offered no words of remorse.

It was Lucy's turn to be bitter, but she managed to keep her tone measured. "All right. There's not much to tell. I started to walk down the aisle, then Tyler announced to the world that the wedding was off. And that's it—my sad story. I hate men, and I think being a bastard must run in your family." She walked briskly into the castle then ran to her room, where she closed the door and breathed deeply while catching her breath. Then she sat on the edge of the bed and stared blankly at the wall. She was not going to cry.

THE MOUNTAINS beyond Lucy's window were shrouded in mist as the afternoon sun gave way to gray dusk. It was this time of day, when the darkness was falling, that she felt most like grieving her loss, and hopeless longing for home overtook her.

Another in a series of periodic knocks at the door resumed.

"Lucy?" It was Rory again. Well, the man was tenacious. But so was she. And she wasn't ready to face him, not yet. She supposed they were even. She might even have hurt him more than he'd hurt her. The difference was, she hadn't meant to hurt him.

A few minutes later, another knock sounded. "Miss Buchanan?"

"Come in, Effie."

With Rory close on her heels, Effie winced and mouthed, "I'm sorry," then set down a tray and made a hasty exit.

He was determined to have his say, and it was his house—well, his castle—so Lucy looked straight into his eyes and waited.

"You have every right to be angry. I lashed out at you because of my own pain, and I'm sorry."

"I was trying to get to know you. I didn't mean to pry."

"Aye. I'm not used to answering questions, at least not about that. We're a bit isolated here, and everyone knows everyone else's business. So I've not had to talk about it in a very long time."

Lucy nodded. "I get that. I'm not exactly eager to talk about Tyler. So why don't we just agree not to talk about things—people—who upset us." She offered her hand to seal the deal.

"First, I must say one last thing."

Her face wrinkled. She wasn't sure she was ready to hear it. "What?"

"I must tell you that your Tyler sounds like—as you would put it—a jerk."

Lucy grinned and shook his hand. "No argument there."

WARM DAUBS of color softened the landscape. Lucy drew in a deep breath of crisp autumn air. What a glorious morning. Rory had said they could use a distraction, so leaving behind the grand Castle Munro, they rode through the glen and up into the hills. Lucy clung to Rory's waist, hoping she would always remember the feel of fresh air on her face and the smell of the grass and the heather as they rode over the deep velvet green of the hills. She felt free there, on horseback in the Highlands of Scotland. Or was it the past that had freed her? Perhaps it was simply the distance from Tyler and the disappointment he'd caused. But after the initial shock and embarrassment, unexpected relief had settled in. Maybe Tyler had been the braver of the two, or the more honest at least, for he'd voiced the same doubts she'd refused to admit even to herself. She still would rather he'd done it before the wedding, not during.

Still, seven years was a long time to be with somebody. Doubts or not, the rejection had still hurt. She would do her best to set those feelings aside for another day when she would be able to think more than hurt. For the moment, she chose to enjoy the fine day. That was all she would let matter right now. She enjoyed even more how it felt to lean against Rory's back and cling to him as they rode across the glen between the stark mountains and on to the cairn.

Fairy cairn was as good an explanation as any for what had brought her to this place. Wormhole, time portal, what did it matter? The result was the same. It was a mysterious and exciting adventure. That fact alone would convince those at home that she was truly delusional, so her story would remain hers alone, never shared. Her time would be better spent concocting a more reasonable explanation for her absence. Then she would set about finding a new job—one without Tyler—so she could get on with her life.

By the time they arrived at the cairn, Lucy felt a slight pang at the thought of never seeing Rory again. No longer leaning against him, she felt cold. He always felt safe and warm. She felt foolish to get lost in such feelings. It was so unlike her.

She slid off the horse and into his arms, and he set her down gently. Poised for a goodbye but unwilling to say it, she looked into his calm brown eyes. Something passed between them in that gaze, and the words "what if" came to her mind.

His eyes shone. "Someday you will be a beautiful bride."

She lifted her palms and looked down at her dress with a smirk. It was wilted and splattered with mud. "I might have to find a new dress."

He smiled, and the warmth in his eyes prompted a twinge of regret. On an impulse, she hugged him. For a moment, they held one another. Her heart pounded until she was sure he would feel it. She lifted her eyes. Dark and open, his eyes drew her in. She could not look away even though she revealed too much simply by looking at him.

"I've got to go," she whispered.

He lowered his arms to release her. She managed to go to the cairn, but she stopped at the entrance. *Just one more look.* Then she walked inside and went to the opposite wall. But that was all it was, just a wall. Rory waited outside. She leaned her forehead on the wall as she ran her fingers down the rocks. She would not be going home, not today. And that realization brought with it a measure of relief. Rory was outside waiting for her. She still had Rory, and he would keep her safe. She soon found herself in his embrace as if it were the most natural thing.

"I'm sorry."

She couldn't speak, so she gave a small nod.

IF RORY HAD HAD plans for the day, he changed them and spent the whole day with her. He described it as a distraction, but Lucy was pretty sure it was an eighteenth-century version of a pity date. But she welcomed the chance for an outing. After a brief introduction to his father, Rory took Lucy for a ride to some of his favorite places. She made a concerted effort to view her time there as a vacation rather than the place she would be stranded for the rest of her life. As a vacation spot, it couldn't have been better. Every direction offered breathtaking beauty, from the bold hills jutting up to the silvery sky to the wide stretch of valley below, which Rory called a strath.

Rory helped Lucy dismount, then he tethered his horse and took Lucy's hand to lead her the rest of the way to the top of the hill overlooking a loch. He spread out a blanket, and they sat for a meal of bread, cheese, and ale. It could not have been more perfect—unless they'd been back in her time. But that was the sort of idle dreaming she'd never indulged in before. This was no time to start.

She fixed her thoughts on more practical matters. "Are there certain conditions you've noticed in which the cairn works?"

Rory hesitated to answer. "I've only seen it twice, when I was a child and when I was with you."

She lifted her chin, vaguely nodding. This was not what she'd wanted to hear.

He peered at her for a moment. "By the time I grew up, I'd given a good deal of thought to my journey through the fairy cairn. As a child, I thought what I'd seen were strange monsters. But as I thought more about it, I became certain it was some sort of passage through time. So when Margery died, I went to the cairn every day for weeks, hoping I might go back in time and change what had happened. I nearly drove myself mad. It never worked, needless to say."

Lucy turned away. His defeated expression was painful to see.

His eyes brightened. "Still, it could happen again."

"I suppose. I'm here, after all, so it can't be impossible."

"No." He turned and looked frankly at her. "But I ken what I've seen, and I ken how I've struggled when the passage was closed to me. And now it appears to go only to the future, so I must let go of the past."

Lucy nodded. He'd lost hope, yet he tried to keep her from doing the same. While the gesture was kind, it was not encouraging.

He peered straight into her eyes. "I promise to take you there every day until you tell me to stop."

A grateful look was all she could manage, for he was willing to go day after day through an exercise he didn't even believe in.

His eyes softened. "Dinnae lose heart, lass. There's a saying here: It's a lang road that's not got a turnin'."

"Okay." She hesitated. "I have no idea what that means."

He laughed. "It willnae be like this forever. Your journey is bound to take a turn for the better."

Lucy's eyes moistened. She wanted to believe him, but he'd left out the possibility that the road could take a turn for the worse.

Rory gave her an encouraging smile then began to pack up the remains of their meal. "Do you like racing?"

Surprised by the abrupt change of topics, Lucy shrugged. "What? Horses? I don't know."

"Well, we're about to be in one."

"On one horse?"

"Aye, it's a race between us and those clouds to see who reaches home first. There's a good chance they'll win, so we'd best be off."

CHAPTER 5
THE CEILIDH

Rory was in the library behind closed doors for most of the following day, so Lucy wandered about. At first, it was as though she'd gained private admission to one of those castles peppered all over the United Kingdom. But this time, she couldn't grab a coffee from the snack bar, hop back into her rental car, and get on with her life. And with no one to talk to, she began to feel restless.

After a few hours of this, Lucy sat at the foot of the stairs with her chin in her hands. "Snack time." With a renewed sense of purpose, she got up and headed for the kitchen. There, she found a woman with her hair in a kerchief, bent over a mound of bread dough.

"Hi, I'm Lucy." She started to reach out her hand then pulled it back, grinning, when she realized the woman's hands were covered in flour and dough.

"Good morning, Miss. I'm Mrs. MacEddie." She stopped kneading the dough and looked up. "What can I do for you?"

"I didn't mean to interrupt."

Mrs. MacEddie had already grabbed a nearby pottery bowl and coated the inside of the bowl with a dollop of lard. "I just need to put this dough to rest, first." She lifted the large mound of dough and plopped it into the bowl. Then she covered it with a cloth, set it aside, and looked up as she swiped the back of her hand across her forehead. "There now, are you hungry?"

Seeing how hard Mrs. MacEddie was working, Lucy began to feel a bit guilty. "I don't want to be a nuisance, but I was hoping I might stick my head in the fridge for a snack."

"Stick your head in the—"

Lucy interrupted, "Sorry. I meant a snack. I was just looking for a snack."

Mrs. MacEddie's eyes lit with recognition. "Oh, aye. I've got a wee bit of black pudding left over from breakfast."

Lucy's eyes brightened. "Oh, that sounds good."

When Mrs. MacEddie brought it to her, it looked like anything but the pudding Lucy expected. She took a bite, and her eyes opened wide. It had a strange taste, which although vaguely familiar, she could not identify. "What's in this?"

Mrs. MacEddie brushed some hair from her forehead. "Ah, well, let's see. I start with four cups of fresh pig's blood..."

Lucy grabbed some ale and washed down what she could while trying to maintain a pleasant demeanor.

Mrs. MacEddie continued. "Oats, pig fat, an onion, some milk, and I season to taste. I'm sorry, I dinnae measure it, so I cannae tell you exactly."

"That's okay," Lucy assured her.

Lucy ate it and graciously thanked the cook, because that was what one did, but not without a refill of ale to cover the lingering metallic taste.

"Oh, you are hungry, lamb. I've got more."

"No! Thank you!" Lucy dabbed her mouth with a napkin. "That hit the spot. I'm full as a tick." She muttered to herself, "Which also eats blood."

"Suit yourself, dearie," Mrs. MacEddie said as she peeled some potatoes. She glanced up when Effie walked into the room. "Oh, Effie, why don't you go pick some raspberries, and I'll make a nice pie?"

Lucy sprang up. "Need some help?"

Effie glanced down, embarrassed. "Oh no, Miss. You shouldnae be helping me."

"And why not?"

"You're a guest. It wouldnae be proper." Effie gave a questioning look to Mrs. MacEddie.

"Who's to say it's not proper?" Lucy asked.

Effie's eyes widened. "I suppose with the laird ill as he is, it would fall to Mr. Rory."

Lucy joined Effie at the doorway. "You leave Mr. Rory to me."

Mrs. MacEddie gave an ambivalent shrug, and the two were on their way.

Effie entertained Lucy with stories about some of the locals while they filled a basket with berries. They were literally sampling the fruits of their labors on their way back to the kitchen. Lucy smiled at something Effie had said, when she glanced up and saw Rory at a second-floor window.

"I'm hoping he'll be there at the cèilidh tomorrow," Effie said.

"Who, Rory?"

Effie wrinkled her face. "No, Symon—the lad I've been telling you about."

"Oh, sorry. Symon." She nodded, as though she'd even heard what Effie had said about Symon, whoever he was.

Lucy glanced back up at the window, but Rory was gone.

LUCY WAS STOIC, with neither a tear nor a sigh, on her way back from the fairy cairn the next morning. Perhaps if she had wept, Rory might have known how to react. But instead, she was silent the whole way home. The stable boy took the horse, and the two headed back to the castle.

Rory looked about while he searched for something to break the silence. "The weather's been passing fair for this time of the year."

"Oh." She stared off into the distance, distracted.

"Usually by this time, the dreich days have set in."

"Hmm."

Rory frowned. She had been disappointed before by the fairy cairn, but this time, she seemed distracted if not despondent.

"Aye." He nodded to himself and glanced over at her. "So... when the weather gets like that, I just tear off my plaid, do a sword dance in the altogether, and finish it off with a grand leap into the freezing cold loch. It eases the boredom. Not mine, you ken, but the crofters."

"Mm-hm."

"Lucy, have you heard even one word I've said?" The lost look in her eyes when she looked up at him tugged at his heart. "Oh, lass. Come here." He pulled her to him and put strong arms around her. "I cannae give you what you want. But I want you to know that you've a home here as long as you want it."

She buried her face in his chest. "Rory."

"Och, lass. There, now. I ken what you need. We'll get Effie to find you a fine dress to wear, and tonight, I'll take you to a cèilidh."

Effie tied off the last thread of the hem on Lucy's dress. "Now let's see how this looks." She helped Lucy into the dress and arranged Lucy's hair. "Oh, Miss, you look bonnie!"

Lucy smiled. "Do I?"

Effie assessed her with a twinkle in her eye. "Aye, and I dinnae believe I'm the only one who will think so."

Lucy shook her head with a grimace. "I think someone's gotten into the whisky."

Effie's eyes opened wide with alarm. "Oh, Miss, I wouldnae ever do that!"

"I was only kidding."

"If anyone believed that to be true, I'd be put out on my ear."

Lucy was suddenly serious. "I'm sorry. I wasn't thinking. I would never want that!"

"I know." Effie's mood brightened. "Will there be anything else, Miss Lucy?"

"No, thank you, Effie. You've been a miracle worker."

"Och!" Effie grinned and modestly waved off the compliment. "Well, I'd best go get ready myself, or I'll need my own miracle!"

AFTER EFFIE LEFT, Lucy looked down at her dress then took in the four walls of the room. It all still seemed so unreal. Her thoughts were interrupted by a knock at the door.

"Did you forget something?" Lucy swung the door open. "You're not Effie." She found herself face-to-face with Rory. It was a toss-up as to who looked more surprised.

"You look bonnie."

"You've been talking to Effie. She just left here saying the same thing."

"No, I formed that opinion on my own."

Lucy blushed. "I think you two are conspiring to improve my mood. But I'll take a compliment wherever I can get it."

"If you're ever in need, come see me." His eyes swept over her face and her hair.

She smiled. Although she didn't believe him, she enjoyed the way he made her feel. For most of the day, she'd felt sorry for herself, and she'd had enough. Determined to make the best of the evening, she took the arm Rory offered, and they left for the cèilidh.

They arrived at a clearing nestled between two hills, where the cèilidh had already begun. Rory tethered his horse to a tree and returned his attention to Lucy. The last rays of sunlight filtered through the colored leaves, which were losing their battle with darkness. Two or three scattered fires lit the area as a full moon worked its way up in the night sky. Lucy smiled to see Effie dancing with a nice-looking russet-haired young man. From the way Effie looked at him, Lucy was sure that he had to be the Symon Effie had told her about. Lucy was happy to report that he looked equally smitten with Effie.

One of the tenants approached Rory and drew him aside for some sort of man talk he seemed to think would be too much for her ladylike ears. Rory hesitated to leave her, but she waved him on confidently. She was not uncomfortable being alone, but people often assumed that she would be. While she found that in her own time, the attitude was even more prevalent here. At such times, she reminded herself that she was in the eighteenth century, and it wasn't fair to judge people by a standard that some in her own era had yet to achieve. Mrs. MacEddie stopped by for a chat but was pulled onto the dance floor, such as it was, by her husband, whose enthusiasm may have partly been due to the flask that peeked out of his pocket. Lucy envied how happy the couple appeared. They were one of those couples who, after decades of marriage, seemed to share a closely guarded secret for living happily together. She hoped she might find that someday.

In the midst of her reverie, Effie's Symon asked Lucy to dance, no doubt prompted by Effie out of pity for her.

Lucy said, "I'd love to. But I should warn you I don't know how to do any of these dances, so I'll count on you to tell me what to do."

He gave it a good, cheerful effort, but Lucy's lack of

skill at Scottish country dancing did not make it easy. He
kindly endured the two or three times that she stepped on
his toes, but he looked a bit worse for wear after having to
chase after her when she went the wrong way around the
circle. She couldn't blame him for looking relieved when
the song mercifully came to an end. After profuse apologies, Lucy took pity, thanked Symon, and begged off the
next dance. Lucy smiled to see Symon and Effie in the
throes of the next dance. The poor guy had earned it. She
glanced about, wondering where Rory was. When she
couldn't find him, she was surprised by the depth of her
disappointment.

The dance ended, and Rory appeared and asked her
for the next one. She tried to warn him, but he would not
be turned down. He slipped his hand in hers and drew her
close. The next song was slower, affording her more time
to react to directions. She lifted her eyes to meet his and
found trust and confidence. There were times when she
looked at him and felt something timeless, as though he
had been there all along, waiting for her. And yet he'd
come into her life like a wind that surprised her and
threatened her balance. Every look held more meaning.
Every touch made her heart soar. She tried to remember
that she was a modern twenty-first-century woman in
charge of her own feelings and fate. But his warmth drew
her closer and made her feel safe until she feared she might
lower her guard and do something stupid like tell him
how she felt. So she did her best to hide the effect he had
on her.

It helped to have to concentrate on the dance steps,
but Rory even made that a bit easier. He never lost track
of where she was or where she needed to be. When she

made a mistake, he would get her back on course and make it seem more fun for her having erred. By the end of the song, Lucy had found her way through the dance but was lost in a life that wasn't meant to be hers. She looked at Rory, and everything faded in importance, leaving her feeling as though she belonged there. Her feelings for Rory were clouding her thinking. Just this morning, she'd been devastated when she couldn't go back home, yet there she was, letting her heart lead her away from everyone and everything she'd ever known.

She took a step back. "I can't do this."

"You're doing fine!" Rory reached for her hand and drew her back to him.

Once more, she was captivated by his winning smile and easy manner. She smiled, relieved he'd assumed she was talking about her dancing. She had a bad habit of thinking out loud. It used to bug the heck out of Tyler. Oh wow, Tyler. She hadn't thought of him all day.

The song ended, and Rory held on to her hand as if doing so were the most natural thing. He led her along a path between groups of people until they arrived at a clearing. The full moon shone above, and a nearby fire warmed the surroundings. The hills were mere shadows, rising around them as if they'd been put there to guard foolish hearts that dared feel things they weren't meant to.

Rory stopped and turned to face Lucy. "I'm sorry for the trouble it's caused you, but I like having you here."

The tender look in his eyes took her breath away. Those deep eyes that looked so stern at times were fixed on hers, and she felt his gaze in her soul. She began to shake her head slowly. But she'd barely begun to turn from him, when he took her face in his hands and kissed her. With that, she stopped thinking and kissed him right back with all the feelings her logic had tried to tamp down. Voices drew nearer, and Lucy stepped back as a couple walked by. She wasn't sure where to look, let alone what to say to Rory. She knew what to think—that she'd lost more than her mind. She'd lost her heart. It was his even though she'd never intended to give it to him.

What sort of woman walked out of her wedding and into another man's arms? Not a stable one. Regardless of Tyler's rejection, a woman in love couldn't shift gears that fast. No, she was either having a psychotic break, or she was just a bad person. Given the choice, she went with the former.

She looked frankly at him. "We can't do that again."

He reluctantly nodded and gently took her elbow to lead her back toward the others.

They'd only gone a few steps when she stopped and pulled him back so she could kiss him. "I mean it. Okay, just one more." Having barely paused to say that much, she kissed him again.

Rory held her close and brushed his lips against hers. "You're a wee bit bossy," he whispered.

She grinned, but it was short-lived as her ingrained defenses came back to haunt her. She pressed her palm to his chest and took a step backward. "I don't know what I'm doing. This wasn't part of the plan."

He kept a safe distance, but not far enough to keep his fervent gaze from making her heart swell. "My plans all changed when I met you."

She looked downward so she wouldn't reveal how his look affected her. "We both know this was a mistake."

"It doesnae have to be." He reached toward her but drew his hand back as though he'd thought better of it.

The last thing Lucy wanted to do was contradict him. Every instinct and drive in her heart and her body compelled her toward him, but she knew she was headed for a hurt far worse than she'd suffered from Tyler. The more she gave in to her feelings, the more entrenched she would become in this time and this life—Rory's time, Rory's life. Things between them had gone too far already. Her heart was going to ache for the rest of her life if they parted... *when* they parted.

No one knew why the cairn worked, let alone how or when. What if her feelings for Rory were anchoring her not only to him, but also to his time? There had to be some reason why the cairn wouldn't open and let her go back. She'd never been one to believe in magic or luck. She'd never even bought a lottery ticket, so time travel was far from her sphere of thought. And yet, there she was. What she thought or believed didn't matter. The heart was a powerful force. It kept people alive, and it drove their life choices. No matter how science would have people believe that love occurred in the minds and the thoughts, it was felt in the heart. Love was a power that no one could fathom, and yet was there a soul on the planet that hadn't been touched by it? That alone proved its power. Lucy had to be careful to guard against that or anything else that might threaten her chances of going back home—even if it meant letting go of Rory.

"I'm not asking anything of you," Rory said. "I just want to love you."

Lucy slowly shook her head. "I gave in to my feelings. It was selfish of me. I don't want to hurt you. If it makes you feel any better, I'm pretty sure I've hurt myself more." She lifted her eyes and tried to smile at him, but she couldn't. "You don't make it easy for a girl to resist." She looked down and shook her head. "But we can't. Don't you see? There's too much in the way. Tyler, for one. I know that it's over, but I met you on my wedding day. I shouldn't even be feeling like this."

To be honest, the thing that disturbed her the most was that Tyler disturbed her the least. Not that he deserved any loyalty from her, but if she had truly loved him enough to commit her life to him, how could she want Rory? And she did.

He touched her shoulder. "I ken that you've just lost the man that you loved and he hurt you. You need time to heal, and I promise I'll give that to you."

Was time all she needed? With or without Rory, she would have needed more time. So if that made sense to Rory, perhaps she should leave it at that. But that was not all there was to it. Most people found it hard enough to commit for a lifetime to someone who shared a similar life in a similar location. But loving Rory meant giving up everything she'd ever known—every person who had ever meant anything to her. It meant giving up time. Thoughts and emotions soared through her mind. Even now, if she could go home, doing so would be painful for having met Rory. Were they actually discussing the *L* word? So soon? A few days ago, she would have scoffed at the idea of love at first sight, but there she was. Maybe the only reason people didn't believe in it was because they'd never felt it. If that was what this was, that gave her all the more reason to shut this thing down.

So why had she kissed him? Because she had wanted

him then as she wanted him now. She'd had one fleeting thought to hold back, but her impulses had taken over. Protecting herself would have been the right choice, but desire was stronger than logic. Even now, she had no regrets. Had she been sensible, she would never have known how it felt when his lips first touched hers or how the pressure of his fingertips on the back of her neck made her forget everything except how much more she wanted him now than a heartbeat ago.

But now that her reckless heart had opened to him, it could not be undone.

CHAPTER 6
MEMORIES OF LOVE

As they rejoined the others, a couple of crofters offered Rory a drink. Lucy excused herself, hoping a few minutes alone might bring her down from her emotional ledge. She made her way through a small patch of bluebells and leaned against an old oak. The full moon shone through the break in the trees, casting a magical glow, the likes of which could only be found in Scotland. Feelings for Rory aside, this place still filled her with wonder.

"Is that you, Lucy?" At first, the voice sounded like Rory's, but Angus was soon by her side. He grinned and leaned back against the tree. "Has that rogue, Rory, abandoned you?"

"No, Angus. He hasn't." Her answer came out a bit sharper than she had intended. She wasn't usually bothered by his glib demeanor, but at that moment, her emotions were raw.

"Are you feeling all right?"

She could barely mask her impatience. "Yes, I'm fine."

"You don't sound fine."

"And you don't sound like you actually care, which is basically business as usual, isn't it?"

It took a lot to render Angus speechless, but Lucy had done it. He clutched his chest and fell back against the tree with mock pretense as if he'd been shot.

Lucy couldn't deny she'd been harsh. "That was uncalled for. Forgive me."

He grinned, fully recovered, and gave her a knowing look, which he combined with his usual charm. "I dinnae suppose this has anything to do with my brother."

He drew her into his gaze, and she smiled. "It's possible."

"Having lived with him for twenty-eight years, I'd wager a bet that whatever he did was his fault, not yours."

"And you'd lose that bet."

"Oh, lovely Lucy, I cannae imagine you doing anything wrong."

"You have no imagination."

He laughed, and she couldn't help but join in. Angus leaned back, folded his arms, and turned his head toward hers. "Why don't you tell brother Angus all about it?"

"You're too charming by half."

Angus smiled as though he'd heard that comment before. "Aye."

"Which is why you'll get nothing from me."

"Och, lass. Is there nothing I can do to coax you?" He flashed a raffish grin. "Or is there nothing I can coax you to do?"

Lucy swatted his arm. As her light laughter faded, she looked up to find Rory a few feet away, watching.

Lucy straightened, leaving Angus still leaning against the tree trunk. "Rory—"

"We were just talking about you." With a sly smile, Angus nodded to Lucy and walked away.

Rory gripped Angus's arm and forced him to stop. In a low voice, he said, "Have you learned nothing?"

Angus shot a dark look at his brother. "It's not what you think, not that it matters to you."

Lucy joined them. "Rory, what's wrong?" Although the thought occurred to her that he could be jealous, it made so little sense that she dismissed it.

Rory's eyes bored through hers. "I'm leaving. Maybe Angus can see you home."

"Rory—" It was too late. He was walking away. Chasing after him would just cause a scene, so she watched him disappear into the misty darkness. She turned to Angus. "How long a walk is it from here?"

"Dinnae fash, Lucy. I'll not leave you stranded."

RATHER THAN ASK RORY, Lucy missed her daily trip to the cairn and lunched in her room to avoid him. But the sun shone, which was not all that common for this time of the year, so she could not resist sneaking out through the kitchen to go for a walk. She'd been walking for twenty minutes or so when she heard a horse slow to a trot, then a walk.

"Lucy?"

She didn't need to look to know it was Rory. "I'm enjoying my walk. Let's not spoil it." She didn't want to stop and look him in the eye, but the last thing she needed was drama, so she stopped and looked.

Rory drew closer. "I had a talk with my brother this morning. Evidently last night, Angus was just being Angus."

"And I was just being myself. Which leaves you. Who was that?"

He looked down, slowly shaking his head.

"I think that I'm partly to blame," she said. "My behavior—with you—it invited assumptions that just can't be."

His eyes burned through her attempted composure. "Your 'behavior'? We kissed, and you cannae even say it."

She looked down, knowing her eyes would betray her. Her voice was surprisingly calm. "I feel as though I've brought back feelings you'd rather not have." She glanced up to see his response.

A flicker of pain crossed his face. "Aye, I suppose you remind me of what love felt like, and it wasnae all good."

She nodded. "Love's not always easy."

"She never knew that I loved her." His eyes flashed as he turned toward her. "I never had the chance to tell her before Angus—" He stopped himself.

Lucy started to speak but thought better of it.

Rory's eyes had a dark, deadened look. "Angus knew. I told him once that I loved her. A week later, I was on my way out to the stable when they came out, hand in hand, laughing together. Until they saw me. Later on, she found me in a place I once took her to. She said she was sorry. She told me she loved him and he loved her too.

"She didn't understand how easily words came to Angus. They still do. He loves women. Every woman he's ever been with, he loves something about. What he loved about Margery lasted a month. In the end, he broke her heart and mine."

"How could he do that to his own brother?"

"He doesnae ken how not to. He didnae do it to hurt me. But I think, when he saw how I loved her, he looked at her differently. Perhaps he wanted to feel what I felt, and he thought that he'd feel it with her as I had. Dinnae think I excuse him, but I do understand him. I'm certain he thought that I'd never find out, so no one would be hurt."

"So you forgave her."

"Did I?"

"You married her, didn't you?"

He smiled a self-deprecating smile. "Aye."

Lucy studied his face, the strong features with such pain in his eyes. If Lucy's heart hadn't already been aching for him, that look would have done it. "And seeing me talking with Angus brought back all those feelings."

His gaze rested on her with a weight that was heavy to bear. A long while passed before he spoke. "I ken how you feel about me."

"It's not about how I feel. It's about what can't be. My future was never meant to be here."

"Lucy." He put his hands on her shoulders, but she took a step back as if he were poison. And maybe he was —for her.

"There's too much in the way," she said. "Tyler, Margery, you're still angry with Angus, and I want to go home. What's wrong with this picture? It's a miracle we're standing here now."

His mouth twitched at the corner. "But we are. And I

dinnae think we should allow the past to keep us from the future."

"Your future." There was no hope in her eyes. "Mine is somewhere through that cairn."

Rory was better at masking emotions than she was. He looked stoic while, for all her good sense and logic, Lucy still wanted nothing more than to sink against his chest and feel his arms about her. But instead, Rory gave her shoulder a slight squeeze and mounted his horse. "It's growing late. We should be on our way."

LUCY ARRIVED home from her daily pilgrimage to the fairy cairn, went up the stairs, and walked down the hall toward her room.

"Uh-agh!"

Lucy stopped outside of the laird's room. When she heard more guttural noises, she knocked. "Captain? Are you all right?"

He moaned.

"Barron? Nurse Dow?" She tried the door, but it was locked. Hearing her, Rory emerged from his room and was soon by her side. "I heard something," she said. "I think he might be hurt."

Rory called out to his father as he tried the door handle. "Stand aside." He kicked in the door.

They found the laird on the floor by his bed. They rushed to him and helped him back onto the bed. Lucy fluffed up some pillows until he seemed comfortable. "Captain, how did you manage to get out of bed?"

His answer was gruff. "How does anyone get out of

bed? I sat up and then stood. That's when things got a bit hazy."

"You probably fainted," Rory said.

Lucy caught sight of the bedside table containing some medical instruments resting inside a bowl stained with blood.

"Captain, has someone been drawing blood from you?"

"Aye, my jailer, Nurse Dow, fills that bowl twice a day."

Lucy started to smile when he referred to his nurse, but when he mentioned filling the bowl, she was deeply concerned. "Captain, if you don't mind my asking, what exactly is the nature of your illness?"

"Och, well if you must know, I had the bloody flux."

Bloody flux. Lucy knew she'd heard that somewhere, but where? Then it came to her: dysentery.

"I got over it days ago," the captain said. "But I cannae seem to get my strength back."

Lucy rolled her eyes. "It doesn't take a doctor to know that losing that much blood is going to make you dizzy and weak."

"What's this?" The captain's nurse stood in the doorway, hands on hips, eyeing the scene.

Lucy made no effort to hide her annoyance with the nurse's scolding glare. "The captain fell, and we're helping him."

"I've only been gone for a minute or two." She appeared far more concerned about how it reflected upon her than she did for the captain's well-being.

"He's all right now."

Rory's father winced as Nurse Dow readjusted his

pillows. "Now, Captain, you shouldnae be out of your bed."

He cast a knowing look at Lucy. "Aye, well, I'd have preferred falling *into* bed, but as it turns out, I had no choice." He gave Rory an impatient glance.

"You should rest," Rory said. "I'll check in on you later."

Lucy snuck a sympathetic look at the captain. "I should go." She smiled at him but then watched the nurse go to the bedside table.

The nurse picked up a sharp, pointy instrument from the bowl. "Time for your afternoon treatment."

Lucy could only imagine spending day and night with the flinty Nurse Dow. As she was no more eager than the captain to incur the woman's displeasure beyond the scowl that was already pointed at her, Lucy trod carefully.

"What treatment is that?" Lucy asked, suspecting the answer.

With a sideways glance that told Lucy she was only answering her out of a limited supply of patience, Nurse Dow said, "I'm breathing the vein."

"You mean bleeding? Bloodletting?"

"Aye, so you must leave now." She kept a sharp eye on Lucy and waited.

"Oh no," Lucy said. "I can't let you do that. In fact, I insist that you stop." She glanced at the captain. "I'm sorry, but this will only make you worse."

The nurse bristled and turned the force of her unyielding will upon Lucy. "And what gives you the right to order me around?"

Lucy wasn't going to get anywhere with the woman by antagonizing her, so she tried to soften her tone without sounding too patronizing. "Not ordering. I'm suggesting that you stop this course of treatment." She narrowed her eyes at the nurse, who, unused to such challenges, widened her eyes. Then Lucy turned to Rory. "Please stop this."

His questioning look was met with Lucy's certainty. "Where I come from, it's widely acknowledged that not only doesn't this help, but it can lead to dire results. She is literally draining the life out of your father."

"No more treatments," Rory said to the nurse.

The woman bristled and dropped the instruments into the bowl with a clink then folded her arms. "I dinnae ken why I'm here if you won't let me do my job."

"It's nothing against you," Lucy said. "I know that you're doing the best that you can." She didn't actually know that for sure, but it seemed to unruffle some feathers.

Nurse Dow settled down in a chair with her knitting, while Rory and Lucy all but tiptoed out of the room.

AFTER WALKING Lucy to her room, Rory went to the library. There, he found Angus and told him what had happened.

"He's all right?"

"Aye. But you ken that there's been a slight change in Father's treatment."

"Oh?"

"Aye. We've stopped the bloodletting."

"We?"

"Lucy and I."

Angus eyed his brother suspiciously. "You ken, do you not, that as firstborn and heir, I make the final decision in such matters. It's how Father wants it."

"He's still able to make his own decisions, and he agrees."

"Does he? Well, maybe that's because he doesnae like an old cow sticking sharp things into his arm twice a day. But if he needs that to get better—"

"He doesn't."

"And how do you ken that?"

"Lucy told me."

Angus nodded with a glint in his eye. "So our bonnie Lucy's a doctor?"

This angered Rory, as Angus must have expected it would. "No, but she kens things."

Angus practically scoffed. "She kens things."

"Have I ever told you how I met Lucy?"

Angus gave him a wry look. "You know you have not, for I've asked."

"Well, I'll tell you. Lucy came through the fairy cairn."

Angus nearly laughed. "You're not speaking in jest?"

Rory shook his head. "Do you ken when, as children, I told you I'd gone through the cairn to the land of the fairies?"

"Aye. So our Lucy's a fairy?"

"It wasnae the land of the fairies, it was the future— nearly three hundred years from now."

Angus shook his head. "No, that's madness. That's what you're talking. Pure madness."

Rory nodded. "I cannae blame you for doubting."

"Doubting? You're mad as a March hare if you think that she's telling the truth."

"She has no reason to lie."

"Unless she's as mad as you are. Or maybe you're just that much in love."

Rory glowered. "If I were, I wouldnae tell you."

Angus's eyes flickered in reaction to Rory's remark, but he ignored it. "You're asking me to withhold Father's medical treatment—treatment which could save his life—based on the opinion of a woman we barely know... from three hundred years in the future."

Rory leveled a look that would have unsettled a lesser man. "She's certain it would cost him his life. I believe her."

What Rory was asking of Angus was not an easy thing, and he knew it. The fact that Angus wasn't already walking out the door spoke a good deal about his respect for his brother.

Angus walked over to the window and looked out. "From the future... She does speak very strangely."

"Aye, she calls it a New York accent."

Angus looked doubtful. "Well, the old York accent doesnae sound a thing like it." He turned to Rory. "We'll see how he feels tomorrow and the day after that. If at any time he seems worse, we'll resume treatments."

Rory nodded his agreement.

CHAPTER 7
FORGIVE US OUR DEBTS

The gauzy gray sky touched the tips of the mountains as Lucy rode back from the fairy cairn to her erstwhile home, feeling defeated. She had analyzed the cairn until her head ached. What was she not doing that she'd done the first time? Was it the time of day, the weather, what she was wearing, or her state of mind? Well, that was a problem because, after all this, her state of mind was not strong. She was not one to give up, so the more the cairn's magic eluded her, the more determined she grew. It wasn't that she was unused to failing. She'd done that enough. But she'd always pressed on and worked harder to succeed. But in this case, there was nothing to work at. All she could do was keep trying and not give up hope. The latter was the hardest, even for her.

At some point, Rory had stopped saying "I'm sorry" when they returned from the cairn. As they both walked away, he would just take her hand. She never told him how that simple act comforted her. She feared if she did, her whole heart would spill out in a big, ugly mess. No, she wouldn't go there.

The ride back was unusually silent. They rode separately now. Rory had taught her to ride, and she had her own horse, which afforded her more time to think without the distraction of putting her arms about his waist and leaning against him. She did love how that felt, which was why it was better not to feel it. The trips to and from the cairn were a vulnerable time when his touch made her feel less alone, maybe even stronger, while she regrouped. But that same touch sparked a fire that could burn her.

He had never once pushed their relationship after the night they had kissed at the cèilidh. Rory Munro didn't need to be told more than once; he was too proud for that. Not that she faulted him for it. He was so good to her. But he would not beg for anything. It was that pride that made her feel safe with him. He would be by her side as she made her way down this path she had stumbled upon, but he would not ask her for more than she was able to give. What he didn't know was how much she wished that she could give more, for she could not deny that Rory Munro was one of the best things that had ever happened to her.

A FIRE FLICKERED in the carved limestone fireplace and cast a warm glow on the library. In the window alcove, Lucy sat reading by the last daylight in the shortening days before winter.

"Oh good, you're here! I've got something for you."

Rory's eyes were bright, and color still clung to his cheeks from a brisk ride through the chilly evening air. Back from business in town, he carried a package wrapped in paper. As he drew nearer, he untied the string and set it down on the seat beside Lucy. "I thought these might suit you."

He handed her three lengths of cloth, one at a time. The first two were lightweight tartan, one moss green and blue, and the other red with wide blue and green stripes, and the third was a deep-green silk. He watched her examine the fabric.

"They're lovely."

"It's time you had some clothes of your own."

"Thank you." She held and touched the fabric with an admiring but increasingly puzzled look.

"And I thought, too, that sewing might help pass the time."

"Rory, I don't know how to sew." She hated to admit it after he'd gone to such expense for her.

He looked at her as though she'd just told him she didn't know how to breathe. "You cannae sew?"

Lucy shook her head.

Rory tried to process that news. "They dinnae teach that to girls where you come from?"

"No, not to everyone."

"But what do you do in the evenings when you sit by the fire?"

Lucy decided her answer was better left vague. "Oh, sometimes we read books or play games."

"Oh, like chess?"

"Sure." She smiled. Video games would have been too much to explain.

"I see. Well, I'll ask Effie to stitch these up for you."

"I hate for her to have to do extra work for me."

Rory shrugged. "We'll find someone to help with her chores."

"Well, all right, as long as it's no extra work for her."

Rory's eyes shone. "You're a kind lass."

"It's easier than being unkind."

"Aye, so it is." He put his hand on her shoulder and kissed her on the forehead and turned away. "I'll fetch Effie."

Lucy watched while he went to the doorway and instructed the footman to find Effie. Lucy still felt the touch of his lips on her forehead.

MINUTES LATER, Effie and Lucy were in the kitchen, leaning over the fabric, discussing the best use for it. Having finished taking Lucy's measurements, Effie gathered up the material in her arms. Lucy was sitting down for some tea, when lengths of fabric fluttered to the floor.

Effie murmured a hasty "excuse me" and ran outside with her hand over her mouth.

Lucy and Mrs. MacEddie stared at the empty doorway. While Effie had made it out of sight, she had not made it out of earshot.

"Do you think it's something she ate?"

Mrs. MacEddie bristled. "I beg your pardon. It's nothing she had here, I assure you."

Lucy winced. It probably wasn't the best time to explain the concepts of germs and bacteria. "Oh no, I didn't mean *your* cooking, Mrs. MacEddie."

Mrs. MacEddie turned her scowl back to her soup pot.

Lucy bent over the rumpled pile of fabric. "Well... uh... I'll just pick this up and be on my way." She hastened to leave it in a neatly folded pile on the table then made a quick exit before she dug herself in any deeper.

A MUTED THUMP on the front door caught Lucy's attention just as she was about to go up the main stairway. She looked about for the footman, but she was alone. She felt foolish for having looked for a servant. It wasn't as if she'd never opened a door by herself. As she touched the door handle, she heard a grunt. She pulled open the heavy wooden door and gasped. "Angus!"

He collapsed over the threshold in a heap. Blood dripped from his nose as he looked up at her through the one eye that wasn't swollen completely shut. He didn't even look like himself for the swelling and bruising. She dropped to her knees beside him. "Who did this to you?"

He labored to speak. "I owed someone some money."

Lucy looked up and heaved a sigh. "Oh, Angus." She stopped herself from saying more. He didn't need to be beaten up again, this time with words. "C'mon, let's get you inside." She stood and hooked her elbow in his and pulled without success. The footman returned and uttered an initial gasp before regaining his composure. He and Lucy together got him on his feet. Angus hooked one arm about each of their necks, and they practically dragged him into the library to the tapestry-upholstered settee. Lucy sat beside him, while the servants bustled about, caring for Angus and looking for Rory, who was nowhere to be found.

Before long, Rory came in with no jacket and his shirtsleeves rolled up. "Och, my horse threw a shoe, and I had to walk him home. God's wounds, what happened to you?" His initial shock soon turned to disgust as he watched Angus doing his best to smile charmingly at Lucy.

Lucy arranged a wet cloth on Angus's forehead then dabbed with another to finish cleaning the dried blood and dirt from his wounds. That done, she looked up at Rory. There was no sympathy there.

"What is it this time?" Rory asked over his shoulder as he went to the desk.

Angus's answer was barely intelligible. "Card-playing debt."

Rory said to one of the servants, "Get him upstairs." Then he walked to the window and folded his arms until Angus was gone.

Lucy followed Angus upstairs and made sure he was comfortable before marching back downstairs to the library. "Whatever Angus has done, you don't kick a man when he's down."

"Do you know how many times I have relived this scene? If it weren't for me, we wouldn't have the home that we're standing in now. He'd have gambled it all away. And for all I know, he may have just done that too. As soon as I'm able to discuss it without wanting to punch him in the face, I'll get to the bottom of this latest debacle, and once more, I'll bail Angus out of whatever fix he's gotten himself into. Because that's what I do. You dinnae have to like it, but you might consider keeping your opinions to yourself if you're gonnae stay here."

Lucy felt as though the rug had been pulled out from beneath her. She had never seen Rory this angry, and she didn't like being on the receiving end of it. "Oh, I will! I'll keep my opinions to myself as I walk out the door!" Which she did.

Rory calling her name was the last thing she heard when she closed the front door of the house behind her. That was all well and good until she stopped and wondered where she thought she was going.

RORY FUMED for a few minutes before he went after her. With his own horse out of commission, he took Angus's horse and caught up with her about a mile down the road. "And just where are you going?"

"Away from you."

Rory nearly smiled. "Well, you're not doing a very good job of it."

Lucy stopped, heaved a sigh, and said over her shoulder, "Well, you know what they say—if at first you don't succeed, try, try again." She resumed walking.

Rory dismounted and led his horse by the reins as he walked beside her. "I was angry and said things I shouldn't have said. I've hurt you, and I dinnae like how that feels."

Lucy stopped. "That's all that matters, isn't it? How *you* feel."

He seethed with frustration. "How I feel? I have spent the last several weeks setting my feelings aside because of how *you* feel—because that's what you want. You, Miss Lucy Buchanan, get everything that you want."

"Oh, I wouldn't say that. If I got what I wanted, I wouldn't be here!"

He lashed out in return. "But you are. And you might have been lost in the hills or worse if—" He stopped himself.

"Go ahead, say it. If it weren't for you. And I'm thankful. I know that you probably saved my life, and I'll never forget what you've done for me."

The fact that she said it so sincerely made him feel all the guiltier for what he had said. He felt very small at the moment. "I dinnae want your thanks, nor do I want you to leave."

She looked at him with disarming directness. "You can't shut me up."

He raised his eyebrows. God knew he'd found that out on his own.

"Rory, I will not be shushed and set in the corner to tend to my sewing. I can't be like the women you're used to. I can't sew, but I can think. I've got a brain and opinions. I may not always be right, but I've got a right to be wrong—and to voice it."

Rory considered her words for a moment. "All right. But you need to listen to me now before you pass judgment."

"Fair enough."

"There are things you dinnae ken about Angus. I've been cleaning up his messes since we were wee lads. My father's always been blind to his flaws, so you'll have to forgive my lack of patience at hearing the same excuses I've heard all my life."

Lucy nodded and glanced in the direction of the inn.

His eyes crinkled a bit in the corner. "Don't go."

With round eyes, Lucy looked up at him. "I don't want to."

"Ever."

She met his gaze, and he knew there was something between them.

"I don't want to," she repeated, this time in a whisper.

Rory offered his hand, and she took it. Then they took their time on the quiet walk home.

RORY STOOD beside Angus's bed. "How much?"

Rory cursed when he heard the amount. "Are you trying to ruin us?"

"No. It just happened." Angus lay in bed looking like a sad, helpless puppy.

"Dinnae give me that look. This is your estate. Yours. Here I am, second son, doing all I can to preserve your legacy, while you do everything you can to waste it. When the captain finds out—"

"Does he have to?"

Rory had seen that pleading look too many times to be moved. "Aye, he must know. 'Tis his money, and he'll be up and about soon enough to see it himself. I'll not take the blame for you."

"I'm sorry."

He was always sorry. That was the trouble with Angus. Everything, including apologies, came too easily and often too late.

Rory looked at him with piercing eyes. "The next time

you get into a bind, I may not be here, and then, for a change, you can pick up the pieces yourself."

"There willnae be a next time. I swear it."

Rory nodded and left. How many times had he heard those same words?

CHAPTER 8

WHAT IF?

Another of Angus's storms had blown over but not without the captain having to pay off his gambling debts. Angus stayed close to home for a while, although Lucy imagined it was more from lack of funds than by choice. She did her best to steer clear of the family controversy, but in the days that followed, she often heard muffled men's voices behind the closed library doors. She took to reading in a small, seldom-used sitting room with tall windows that made for good reading light.

"There you are!" Lucy smiled and set down her book as Rory burst in and walked over to her.

"Would you mind if I joined you?" he asked.

"Of course not."

His face had lost its cheer, replaced by a thoughtful look that led Lucy to guess that he hadn't just happened upon her. He leaned against the wall by the window where Lucy sat and looked out at the barley that waved as the wind swept through the valley. A cloud darkened part of the field with its shadow as it slowly rolled by. Rory pulled a chair over and sat down beside her.

"Rory?" There was no point in trying to ignore how strangely he was behaving.

"Have you enjoyed your stay here?"

She wanted to laugh because he sounded as though he were checking her out of a hotel. "Yes! You've all made me feel welcome. I don't know what I'd have done without you."

He leaned closer. "I'm glad. I ken how this must have been for you. Coming to a strange place cannae be easy."

With half a nod, she agreed.

"I wish I could have made it easier for you."

"Easier?" She shook her head. There were times when he made her forget what had gone wrong in her life. Lately, all that it took was his gaze for everything to feel right. How much easier could he have made it?

He ran his finger along the carved grooves in the arm of the chair. "Have you thought about what you'll do if you cannae go home?"

Lucy took in a sharp breath as the thought struck. Was he going to ask her to leave?

"What is it, lass?"

"Nothing." It was anything but.

Rory looked far too grave. "My father has recovered, thanks to you."

"I'm glad." They shared a warm smile.

Rory continued. "And now with Angus being... well, Angus... the captain has grown quite busy, thinking and planning."

"That's good, isn't it?"

"Aye, for the most part, it is."

When the pause that followed had gone on long enough, Lucy said, "But..."

"He seems to think that what Angus needs is a wife."

Lucy's tension dissolved. She'd misread the whole thing. This was not about her. Rory just needed someone to talk to. She could relax, and they could just talk.

"Knowing Angus, getting him married off might be a hope that the captain will have to abandon." Rory grinned, but it was only in passing.

"But as we discussed it, the thought came to me that I might marry as well."

"No!" Lucy covered her mouth. Her response had come out before she'd thought better of it.

With a sharp turn, Rory looked at her, surprised by her reaction. "No?" He lowered his eyes.

Lucy looked about as though the right words could be found flitting about in the air. "What I meant was, 'No way!'" She smacked her palms on her knees and smiled brightly.

It was his turn to stare blankly.

She shrugged. "It's how we talk in my time. It's a good thing. It means I'm happy for you."

He peered at her with a confused frown.

The bright, confident face she'd perfected for client presentations was losing its gusto. "Of course you should marry. Is it someone I know?"

Shifting his weight, he leaned back in his chair and folded his arms as he scrutinized her. "She's from away. I've always found her quite lovely."

Lucy nodded, finding it harder and harder to keep her expression appropriately neutral.

"She's smart, kind to animals." His brow creased.

"I've never seen her with children. That might be a problem." His mouth twitched at the corner. "Och! I'm sure we can work through it."

Lucy caught herself frowning and stopped. Maybe this was why women got Botox injections—for moments like this.

"In truth, I've enjoyed every moment I've ever spent with her," Rory said. "So I've decided it's time."

"Time?"

"To ask her."

Lucy's eyebrows lifted a little too much as she smiled. "Well, thank you for, uh, sharing. I hope you're both very happy." She looked at her bare wrist, forgetting she wasn't wearing a watch. "I've got a... thing. I completely forgot. Excuse me." And that was all she could manage before she stood to make her escape.

He stood, blocking her way. "Lucy."

Well, that was it. Trembling would not be the worst of it. Tears threatened to follow. "Please let me go." She looked down, knowing that one more look at him would dissolve what was left of her composure.

Rory didn't move a muscle, and with so many, that was quite an accomplishment.

She lifted her gaze as far as his shoulders. "Rory?"

When he didn't answer, she looked up to find his eyes fixed on hers.

"Lucy, I was speaking of you."

If her life hadn't been such a mess, the love in his gaze would have melted her to a tartan-covered puddle.

He searched her eyes. "Is there a chance you could... love me?"

A chance? The last thing she needed to say was the

truth—that she couldn't imagine a life without him, even though she knew that they couldn't be together. The deeper her love grew, the more it would tear her apart to go home without him. "How can we talk about love or a future? I don't even know if I'll be here tomorrow. We've got to face facts. It just can't be." She went on as if she might convince herself. "How could I love you?"

"How could I not love you?"

Her knees were about to give way, but it was the soft touch of his hand on her cheek that did her in. She leaned against him to steady herself.

And to kiss him.

When he clutched her against him, she whispered, "I've tried so hard not to love you."

A wistful smile teased his lips. "And how did you fare?"

She shook her head. "I suck at not loving you."

"You what?"

Lucy grinned. "It means... Never mind. Kiss me now. I'll explain later."

CHAPTER 9
THE UNINVITED GUEST

Lucy held the captain's arm as they walked into the library then got him situated comfortably by the fire with a book and a quilt to warm him. She took a seat in a chair on the opposite side of the fireplace and gazed at the captain, who was now immersed in his reading. She was gratified by how quickly his health had improved after the bloodletting had stopped.

The late-afternoon light poured in through the tall windows and brightened the room. This was not a bad life, she had to admit. Within a few weeks, she'd grown used to the loss of some modern conveniences, but she still missed the people—her mother, mainly. She missed her friends too, but they had their own lives and would manage without her. But her mother had been her only parent as well as her best friend. She'd had Lucy in college after her father was long gone. It was always the two of them versus the world. And they'd won. They'd struggled along the way, but it had all worked out—well, except for the wedding. That hadn't gone all that well. But her mother had instilled a strength and independence in her that had seen Lucy through that.

But now there was Rory. One moment, she was euphoric, and the next—when her brain started to function again—she despaired. Each contingency that came to her mind had some sort of sorrowful sacrifice attached. What if? She had to stop prefacing every waking thought with what if. For in truth, there was no way of knowing.

Restless, Lucy set her book down and went to sit by the window. Angus came in, still looking battered, but his bruises were fading, and he was moving about with more ease.

A flutter of fabric outside caught Lucy's eye. She recognized the dress. "Effie?" she whispered. She was walking away in the middle of the day, wiping her eyes. Lucy knocked at the window, but Effie didn't hear her. "Something's happened."

The captain glanced up at Lucy and Angus then returned to his reading, while Angus picked up a book and leaned comfortably back. Although neither of them seemed to care, Lucy did, so she rushed from the room to go help the maid.

A rush of cool air struck her as she burst through the doorway and called out to Effie. The girl turned and glanced back but kept going. Lucy called out again.

"I'm sorry, Miss," Effie cried. "I must go."

Baffled, Lucy went back inside. "What's happened to Effie?"

The captain shook his head. "I dinnae ken, lass."

Angus looked at her with a blank expression.

Lucy shook her head. It didn't make sense. She went

back outside, this time to the stable, where she found Rory and the groom, who stood looking at Rory's horse.

Rory said to the groom, "He's got a new shoe, but when the shoe came loose, he cut this leg here." They bent to examine the wound.

Rather than wait for Rory to finish what he was doing, Lucy went back outside to continue her search for Effie. As she left, Rory took one look at Lucy and excused himself to go talk to her. Once he was outside, she told him what she'd seen. "Why would she leave like that in the middle of the day?"

"Are you sure she wasn't going on an errand?"

"What sort of errand would upset her like that?"

"I dinnae ken."

"Neither does your father or Angus. But something has to have happened."

"If my father or Angus didn't send her away, I cannae imagine why she would leave on her own." He shrugged, at a loss for an explanation as much as she was.

"What can we do? We can't just leave her out there."

"She doesnae live far from here. If you like, we can go calling tomorrow."

"Thank you, Rory."

He gave her that warm smile that always gave her hope that everything would be fine, even when she couldn't imagine how it possibly could.

THE FOLLOWING MORNING, they were all seated at a breakfast of cheese, scones with butter and jam, and a mixture of curds and butter called gruitheam. Lucy was watching the others to see whether they spread the concoction on scones or just spooned it up and ate it, when Rory turned to her.

"After breakfast, let's go for a ride. We can call on Effie if you like."

Angus glanced up but returned his attention to his breakfast.

Lucy's eyes shone as she met Rory's gaze. "I would love that." She hadn't stopped worrying about her distraught friend.

Before Lucy could get out a thank-you, there was a loud pounding and scuffling in the hall. The doors flew open, and in walked a man not terribly tall, with broad shoulders, rough hands, and a face flushed with anger. His steel-gray hair shook as he glanced about until his eyes settled on Angus. He took a step forward, but the butler stepped between them.

Angus started to rise in defense, but the captain reached over and put a hand on his son's arm with subtle restraint. After a sharp look at his father, Angus settled back in his seat, but Lucy noticed him running his fingers over the indented pattern carved into the oak hilt of his dirk.

Captain Munro regarded his uninvited guest with a furrowed brow. "Donald."

"I beg your pardon, Laird, but your son"—he paused in a failed attempt to stifle his rage—"has ruined my Effie."

Rory answered Lucy's questioning look with a raised eyebrow, then he leaned back and observed Angus with narrowing eyes.

Angus calmly eyed Effie's father with a curious squint as though the man were a trifling bother.

"This is a serious charge that you're making," Captain Munro said.

Donald nodded. "Aye, and 'tis true, or I wouldnae be standing here now." He scowled at Angus. "What're you going to do about it?"

"Donald, this is hardly the time," the captain said. "When we've finished our meal—"

Donald tightened his fists at his sides. "I wasnae able to finish my breakfast this morning before my daughter ran outside to get sick."

The sight flashed through Lucy's mind of the time Effie ran out of the kitchen to get sick outside. It made sense now but left Lucy with a sinking feeling.

Angus spoke up for the first time. "As I recall, at the céilidh some weeks back, I saw her with that farm lad she's been keeping company with."

"Oh, aye. I started to go to him first, but she told me it wasnae his fault. She said you're the father."

"Did she? She's quite quick to blame. And given the choice, how convenient that she chose the one with money."

"Money or not, you've defiled my daughter."

"You cannae prove that."

Donald nodded vehemently. "I ken that you paid her off. She told me that too."

"Did she?" Angus asked with a skeptical smirk.

"Oh, aye, after I beat it out of her."

Lucy sharply inhaled, about to protest, but Rory reached under the table and gripped her hand. She flashed him a look, but he countered with a look of caution that she did not receive well. Still, the exchange gave her time to calm down enough to ask, "May I see her?" She was acutely aware of Rory's penetrating stare, so she avoided looking anywhere near his direction.

"No one will see her in this shameful state," Effie's father said.

That was it. She was done with diplomacy, manners, and Rory's discretion. She could not let this go. "But you can't keep her locked away!"

Rory exhaled and leaned back in his chair with a resigned look of one watching an impending train wreck.

Captain Munro cleared his throat. "We all need some time to absorb this new turn of events. I give you my word that we'll all reflect on this situation, after which, I'm sure we can come to an agreement."

"Agreement?" cried Donald. "I'm sure we can agree that she's pregnant and that it's your son's." He stormed out muttering, "Agreement, my arse. We'll see soon enough when the bairn comes."

They all watched Donald storm down the hallway. When he was far beyond earshot, Lucy whirled to glare at Angus. "Angus, how could you?"

He looked into her eyes plainly and shrugged. "The usual way."

Captain Munro picked up his fork. "We'll not talk of such things at the table. Angus, Rory, I'll see you in the library after we've finished our breakfast."

"She's my maid and my friend," Lucy said. "Someone needs to speak up on her behalf."

The captain lowered his fork. "I'll not talk of such things in the presence of ladies. This is a family matter." His expression, while polite, forbade further discussion.

Lucy gave Rory a frustrated look, but he just lifted his eyebrows and turned to finish his meal.

BEHIND CLOSED DOORS, the discussion continued. Lucy stood outside the door, not caring if anyone caught her eavesdropping. This treatment was an age-old wrong that had been done to women, who bore all the guilt for what took two to create. She wanted so much to go to Effie and give her much-needed support, but Rory had convinced her that Effie would wind up paying the price if Lucy went against her father's wishes. So she helplessly stood outside one door while barred from another.

The outcome of the family meeting was to send Effie's family more money to compensate for their inconvenience.

Lucy stood by the stairway and whispered to Rory, "Inconvenience?"

"Aye, lass. I ken that it might be different in your time."

"Oh, I don't know that it's all that different. Men can still be unprincipled jerks."

He met her outrage with even tones. "You cannae change my world any more than I can change yours."

"Maybe not on my own, but that doesn't mean I should stand by and allow injustice to go on without standing against it. The world is made up of small pieces, and those pieces can change one by one. In my time, the world has changed for the better because people stood up against wrongs. You can't know how frustrating it is to step backward like this."

Rory straightened his posture. "As much as you may loathe this backward home of mine, you'd have been far worse off with most other men who might have happened upon you alone on the road."

His chastising expression was not lost on her. "Point taken. I do appreciate what you've done for me, but that doesn't help Effie. However unintentional or unwanted that baby might be, Effie is carrying Angus's child, your niece or nephew and the captain's grandchild. Angus is equally to blame, and I'm being generous there. Yet he appears to have no consequences for his actions. You all allow him not only to shirk his responsibility, but to dump it on Effie. She doesn't deserve to be treated like that—to be paid off and sent away, where she'll pay the true price for the rest of her life. Meanwhile, Angus continues to do as he pleases, and the rest of you call it an inconvenience. It's not an inconvenience; it's a baby. And this is infuriating!"

"Your fury is misplaced on me. I cannae undo all the wrongs Angus does. I can only try to pick up the mess that he's left."

She looked up at his soft brown eyes and soothing expression and felt at least some of her anger subsiding. "I guess. Maybe you're right—partly. I'll agree that you shouldn't have to pay for what Angus has done."

He smiled. "I'm well-practiced at it."

She put her hand on his and squeezed it. Having vented her anger, she felt better even though she had unfairly dumped it on Rory. "But poor Effie. Surely there must be something more we could do than to leave her in that stifling croft for her father to beat at will."

Lines in Rory's forehead deepened at the mention of

Effie's beating. "I'll see if there's a place—perhaps an empty croft somewhere she could stay."

"Or a room here?"

His eyes settled on hers. "Perhaps."

At that moment, she threw away all her restraint and put her arms around his neck. He held her close in return. The feel of his body against hers sent all further thoughts from her mind, including those of protecting her heart. She looked up. Her lips parted to thank him, but no words came out as her gaze slowly fell to his mouth.

In the back of her mind was the nagging apprehension that any day she might walk back through the cairn. The first time, it had been with a broken heart, and the next time would be no different.

But by the time she reminded herself what a bad idea it was, they were already kissing.

CHAPTER 10

MATTERS OF HONOR AND DUTY

L ucy stood between Angus and the door. He was dressed in his finest and ready to leave for another evening of drinking and gambling. But Lucy was determined.

He lowered his chin and lifted his eyes with wry boredom. "This is hardly the time."

"Oh yes, it is. I've been trying to speak with you all day."

He looked down, unable to deny that he'd been avoiding her.

She pulled up straight and lifted her chin. "It's time you face up to your responsibility. You can't leave Effie to bear the brunt of this alone."

Angus looked at her frankly. "She's been well paid for her trouble."

"Her trouble?" Lucy rolled her eyes. "Oh, I wish men would have to go through labor. The illegitimacy rate in this century alone would dramatically drop."

"What?" Angus asked, squinting.

"She's carrying your heir."

"Ah, but there's a difference between a bairn and an heir. An heir is legitimate; that child is not."

"Then make it so! For once, Angus, do something right."

A threatening shadow darkened his eyes. "Take care who you order around."

Her eyes flashed. "Someone needs to tell you, so it may as well be me. Your brother has been running this estate and covering for you for so long, it's just business as usual for him. And your father, God bless him, has a soft spot for you that has spread to his brain and affected his judgment. Meanwhile, you're drinking and gambling away your family's assets, not to mention your life. If you're determined to destroy your own life, I won't stop you, but I will not let you do it to Effie, not to mention to Rory."

Angus leaned back, wide-eyed. "Rory's a big boy. Aren't you, Rory?"

Lucy turned around. How long he'd been standing there, she didn't know. But from the look on his face, long enough.

"Aye. And she's right."

Angus stared back at Rory with an unreadable expression then regained his equanimity and grinned with his usual charm. "Well, with that settled, I'm off." He paused in the doorway and turned. "Maybe Rory could marry the wee bastard's mother. It wouldn't be the first time, would it, Rory?" Angus left, closing the door firmly behind him.

Rory's eyes flashed with rage as he threw open the door and called after his brother. "So you could kill her too?" He sprang forward.

"Rory." Lucy tried to grab hold of his arm, but he yanked it away.

"Stay out of it."

Lucy stood in the doorway and watched as Rory caught up with Angus and landed two punches that left Angus on the ground, panting and swiping the back of his hand over his bloodied nose.

"It's your turn, Angus. And I'll see that you take it."

Lucy ran past Angus and caught up with Rory in the stable. "Where are you going?"

"To Effie's." He stopped and stared at his horse's bandaged leg, then told the stable boy, "Saddle Angus's horse."

Lucy put herself squarely in front of him so he could not ignore her. "What are you going to do?"

Leaving the boy to saddle the horse, he took hold of her elbow and led her outside. It was starting to rain, so they stood under the eaves. "I'll bring her back here and see that he marries the girl."

"Out of spite?" She shook her head. That was not what she'd wanted. Once more, Effie would bear the brunt. Lucy didn't want to see the girl given a home out of anger, where she would be resented if not reviled.

Rory looked at her with sternness that shocked her. "You started this. It's too late to complain about how it turns out."

"What did Angus mean about you marrying her?"

Rory chuckled bitterly.

"You accused him of killing your wife."

His eyes darkened. "Why can you not leave it alone?"

"I'm too invested."

"Och, sometimes you speak, and all I hear is rubbish. I dinnae ken you mean. I dinnae ken whether I want to."

"I mean that if there's to be anything between us, I need you to be honest with me. What happened to Margery?"

Rory's jaw tensed, and he looked about as if caged. Then harsh eyes landed on hers. "She died giving birth to Angus's child."

Lucy needed a moment to absorb what he'd said, but once he'd begun, there was no stopping him.

"One day, after Angus had discarded her and moved on, she came to me. Desperate. With child. She begged me to talk to Angus. She'd already tried. He insisted he wasn't the father. She said there'd been no one else, but he called her a liar and sent her away."

Lucy was too stunned to speak.

"So I married her."

"Oh, Rory." Whatever character Angus lacked, Rory had twofold.

"Dinnae look at me like that. I did it because she was with child not because I forgave her. I hated her, but I just didnae hate her enough to send her away." He shook his head and stared off into the distance. "Then she died having Angus's baby. I'll never forgive him for that."

Rory glanced inside the stable as the groom approached with his saddled horse. "Would you make sure a room is prepared in case I'm able to bring her back here?"

"Of course."

Rory rode off moments later and was soon at full gallop on his way to Effie's.

Lucy walked into the house, feeling as though her

whole world were crumbling about her and she was to blame, at least partly. She'd brought old pain back to life and stirred up tension between the two brothers. But she had to live with herself, and allowing Effie to be shooed away like some wayward mutt was something she couldn't let go unaddressed.

She turned her thoughts to more immediate matters. After arranging a room for Effie, she considered Captain Munro. He would need to be told what they had planned. She didn't have to look far to find him. As she neared the library, she heard Angus and Captain Munro in a quiet but heated discussion. She did an about-face. This was not a good time.

She wasn't sorry for what she'd said or done. What she'd said had come from the heart. Lucy had been one of those bastards Angus had spoken of with a sneer. She'd seen how hard it had been for her mother to raise her alone. She could only imagine how much harder it would be for Effie.

Lucy walked into her bedroom and closed the door. Why had she come to this time? It certainly hadn't been by choice. Had her life not already been complicated enough? She went to the window and looked at the shades of green gently draping the hills and the glen. Why, when surrounded by such staggering beauty, must life be so cruel? And for all she knew, a similarly harsh judgment could fall upon her. She was there at the Munros' will and their mercy. After what she'd said to Angus, he would be within his power to cast her out with or without Rory's consent.

Rory rode along the pass through the tall Highland hills to the croft where Effie lived with her father. He thought he had grown too hard for Angus to hurt him again, but then Lucy's words brought back the way he'd felt on that long-ago day when Margery had come to him, so desperate.

She'd wronged him, and she'd known it, but it hurt to see her like that. In her way, she loved him. He saw it in her eyes through the sadness. But she loved Angus more, and her leftover love seemed to mock him. He couldn't bear to see it. He wanted to hate her and send her away, but he couldn't. So he did the right thing by marrying her, but then he punished her by withholding even the smallest bit of comfort or warmth.

When she lay in his arms, dying, he begged for forgiveness. And she gave it to him, but his remorse was too late to help. By the end of the day, she and the baby had been dead, and he may as well have been.

If Angus was repeating the mistakes of his past, then Lucy had forced Rory to remember not only the pain of the past, but the love of the present. Since he'd met Lucy, he felt something he'd given up on: hope. He'd begun to think of a future that wasn't alone. If she couldn't get back to her home, he hoped to convince her that her future was there with him.

In the meanwhile, he would bring Effie back to the castle and make sure she was cared for, with or without Angus's help. The bairn she carried was a Munro, and that child would be properly cared for.

A shot rang out from the hills. Rory looked up to see where it had come from, then drops of blood fell to his hands, and the world went black.

CHAPTER 11

THE PRICE OF PASSION

L ucy was in her room in a chair by the window when she heard a gunshot. Hunters. She shook her head and went back to her book. She'd been staring at words without reading until she finally gave up and set it down. She paced back and forth in front of the fire then decided that, as restless as she was, a walk would do her more good than a book. She was on her way downstairs when she heard the stable boy breathlessly talking to the butler.

"I heard a gunshot, then Mr. Munro's horse came back on its own."

Lucy rushed down the stairs. "Which Mr. Munro?"

"Master Rory is missing," the butler said before continuing his search for the captain.

Lucy bent down and held the boy's shoulders. "Which way was he going?"

As soon as he told her, she was on her way out the door but then stopped to consider. What if he couldn't get on a horse on his own? She couldn't hoist him up by herself. It had rained all afternoon, and the boggy ground was too soft for carriage wheels. Did they even have a carriage? She hadn't bothered to notice. Her mind raced. He would have to be brought back on horseback. The only men around were the elderly butler, the still-weak captain, and Angus.

Lucy hurried to Angus's door and knocked loudly. When she got no response, she pounded until her fist hurt.

Through the door, she heard Angus's voice. "God's teeth, what's all the fuss?" He opened the door, whisky glass in hand.

"Angus, I think Rory may have been shot."

"What?"

"We don't have time to talk now. We've got to go get him."

Despite his slow and deliberate speech, Angus slurred most of his words. "Lucy, I'd like to help, but I cannae." He leaned closer as if telling a secret. "I've had a few drinks."

"I don't care. The cold rain will sober you up. Now, come on."

She hooked her arm in his and dragged him to a chair. On the way, he stumbled but regained his balance with Lucy's support. She struggled to put on his shoes.

He leaned forward and grinned. "You know, most women pull my clothes off."

She rolled her eyes as she finished then stood.

"Slow down, lassie." He smiled and reached for her, but she took the extended arm with a yank and pulled him out of the chair.

"For once, would you think of someone else? Angus, your brother needs you. Let's go."

Through driving rain, they rode, trying to see through the mist that obscured everything beyond a few feet ahead. It got so bad, they had to get down and walk for fear of not seeing Rory and trampling him with their horses.

Lucy followed Angus closely. "How do you know where to go?"

"I've spent all my life here. Between that and the moonlight, we'll find our way somehow."

They inched along, aided by occasional patches where the drifting mist thinned.

Angus talked most of the way, which helped assure Lucy of his presence beside her through the thickest fog. "It's not like Rory to let a horse throw him, especially my horse, which has brought me home when I was three sheets to the wind."

"Angus, shh." She reached over and clutched his sleeve. "Rory?"

Angus stopped, and they listened but were met with silence.

"I'm sure I heard something." She called out again. "Rory? Please, Rory? Where are you?"

"Lucy, is that you?"

"Effie?"

"Over here. I'm here with Rory."

They stepped carefully, following Effie's voice until a

clear patch revealed Rory in a heap on the ground with Effie beside him.

"Rory!" Lucy knelt next to him. "What happened?"

Effie had wrapped a bandage around Rory's head. He was conscious but disoriented.

Agitated, Effie said, "When my father came back from seeing you"—her troubled eyes flickered toward Angus— "he took his rifle and left. I followed him and watched him climb up the hill. I didnae ken what he was doing until I saw Angus's horse. I ran and called out to Rory, but he fired. Rory's horse reared, and he fell."

Lucy started to ask why he thought Angus would be there, but what evening didn't Angus ride by on his way to the inn?

"He thought it was Angus. I did too." She looked up at Lucy. "I'm sorry. I couldn't move him. I didnae ken what to do, so I stayed here with him."

Lucy gripped Effie's shoulder. "That's okay. Look at me. We have to help Rory now."

Effie calmed herself as much as could be expected. "Aye."

He couldn't ride on his own, and the three of them tried but couldn't hoist him onto Angus's horse. So Lucy mounted her horse, while Effie and Angus managed to get Rory on the horse behind her. Then Angus tore a strip of Rory's plaid and tied them together at the waist to keep Rory from falling.

Angus looked at Effie. "Go home, lass."

"No," Lucy said before Effie could move. "Angus, her father has already beaten her and shot Rory. You can't be so cruel as to send her back there."

Maybe if he'd been sober, he might have protested, but Angus looked at Effie and said, "C'mon, then."

The girl hesitated, brow furrowed.

Angus reached out his hand. "There's no other way but with me."

Effie grasped his hand, and he pulled her up behind him. They rode back slowly through the mist at an agonizing pace, but they made it home and got Rory to bed.

FEARING THE WORST, Lucy had left instructions with the butler before they had left to call for the doctor, so he was waiting there when they arrived home. While he tended to Rory, the others waited in the library. Angus slouched in a chair by the fire while Lucy paced and tried not to unload her resentment on Angus. There would be time for that later. Effie had chosen to escape to the kitchen, where Mrs. MacEddie provided her with tea and comfort.

"I never meant to hurt anyone," Angus said as he stared at the fire.

Lucy didn't even bother to look at him as she spoke. At that moment, the less she saw or heard Angus, the better. "You know, Angus, I believe you. The thing is, it doesn't matter. By the time you're done with them, people hurt just the same."

The doctor came in. "It's only a flesh wound. All the blood made it look worse than it was. He's lucky."

The rush of relief was almost too much for Lucy. She trembled but held it together.

"Keep him in bed," the doctor told Angus. "He needs to rest. If there are any changes, send for me. Otherwise, I'll come back in a few days to see how he's doing. Oh, and I looked in on your father. Rory's injury came as a shock, but he's resting. He should be fine by tomorrow."

While Angus thanked the doctor and walked him to the door, Lucy rushed to the kitchen and shared the good news on her way up the servants' stairs to see Rory. He was sleeping, so she pulled up a chair and sat beside him with no plans to go anywhere anytime soon.

In the stillness of his room, all the tension and worry came out, and she silently wept. She hadn't shed a tear since arriving, but now it came out, and she didn't try to stop it. She sniffed.

"There's a handkerchief in that first bureau drawer over there."

She looked over to find Rory smiling at her.

"I didn't mean to wake you."

He pointed toward the bureau. "Go."

She smiled with relief and retrieved the handkerchief. As she sat beside him, he said, "Dry yourself, and then you may throw yourself on me, in that order, please."

Lucy laughed as she dried her eyes and her nose. Then she took his hand in both of hers. "The doctor said it was only a flesh wound."

"Aye, enough blood and mess for a good deal of sympathy."

"Well, you must be feeling all right."

In hushed, conspiratorial tones, he said, "Oh, aye. Just a wee headache."

Lucy smiled, and as she did, she knew that everything in her heart must have shone through her eyes, but she didn't care. She'd nearly lost him, but he was alive, and he soon would be well.

ALTHOUGH HIS HEAD wound bothered him, Rory insisted on being up and about the next day. Angus, on the other hand, made himself scarce. He wasn't missed, at least not by Lucy. The captain, who was fully recovered, sat at the desk, looking over the ledger. The few times Lucy glanced his way, he looked serious, but she assumed that was his normal expression when poring over estate numbers. Lucy was content where she was, beside Rory, reading to him while he lay reclined, eyes closed, with a headache.

The butler quietly walked over to the captain and whispered something. The captain frowned but stood and followed the butler out of the room. A few minutes later, the captain returned with the constable close behind him.

With effort, Rory sat up.

"We've apprehended Donald Vass, the man who shot you."

"Aye?"

"What will happen to him?" Lucy asked.

The constable turned to Lucy. "He'll stand trial, and if he's found guilty, I imagine he'll be transported to the colonies or Australia."

The captain nodded approvingly.

Lucy did not relish the idea of such a harsh sentence for Effie's father. But she thought of how he had beaten Effie when he'd learned she was pregnant. He'd gone straight from beating his own pregnant daughter to lying in wait to shoot Angus. He had wound up shooting the wrong man and then fled. Those were all choices he'd made on his own, and there were consequences for them. He was lucky he hadn't killed anyone. They were all lucky, most of all Rory.

As THE SILVERY afternoon sky cast soft light through the library windows, Angus ventured into the room. His first stop was on the opposite side of the room, where the captain sat at his desk. They spoke in hushed tones, too quiet for Lucy to overhear. When they'd finished, Angus ambled over and sat beside Rory. "I'm sorry to you both. I said things I shouldn't have said, and I didnae mean them."

Lucy found Angus convincingly contrite, which took her by surprise. Rory's reaction was different. Considering what he'd been through, he accepted Angus's words with such ease, she could only presume they'd been through this type of apology before. Perhaps Rory was simply far better than she. There was such a dark history between them, but the bond between brothers was strong.

"I'm most of all sorry that you took a shot that was clearly intended for me," Angus said.

Rory's mouth turned up at the corner. "Well, I'll not borrow your horse again, that's for certain."

Angus laughed. "There's a lot to be said for walking."

Lucy squeezed Rory's hand. "We could have lost you."

Angus cleared his throat. "You could've lost me too." His eyes crinkled at the corner.

She reached over and squeezed his hand. "But you're here, aren't you?"

"Thank you for noticing," Angus said with an impish grin. He leaned toward Rory. "She loves you, you know."

Lucy couldn't help the smile that bloomed.

Rory gazed at her. "I was hoping she might after all the trouble I've gone through to get her attention."

Lucy was thoroughly flustered. She wasn't sure what to say or do, so she did what she always fell back on. She turned the attention away from herself. "So, Angus, what are your plans?" she asked quietly.

That line of questioning had the effect she had hoped for. Rory's smile faded as he turned to Angus.

"I haven't any. I find life more palatable that way." He was trying to be flippant, but he failed miserably.

Lucy's eyes fixed on Angus. "I'm sure Effie would also have found her life more palatable than it is at the moment, but any choice either of you had is long gone now."

Angus folded his arms and said slowly, "It's different for her."

"Yes," Lucy said. "She's got to carry your baby and give birth to it. All you have to do is just be there."

Angus's eyes darted about, but he said nothing.

Lucy looked at Rory, who had been very quiet. Beads of sweat covered his forehead. "Are you all right?" she asked, alarmed.

"Aye. I'm a bit too close to the fire." He sat up and paused, touching his head with a wince. "I think I'll go lie down." He stood up with Lucy's arm hooked in his. He only managed a few steps before collapsing in her arms.

"Angus!" Lucy called, but he was already there, holding Rory up while bringing him back to his seat.

Lucy put her hand to his feverish forehead. She lifted the bandage to look at his wound. It was swollen and red. She wanted a doctor to see him, but these doctors wouldn't be able to help him. It didn't take a medical doctor to know that he had an infection. If it went untreated, he could die. With her layperson's knowledge, she did what she could. She cleaned the wound with whisky and put cool compresses on him. But by morning, he showed no improvement. If anything, he seemed worse. His breathing was labored, his pulse was fast, and he was beginning to murmur delirious nonsense.

She got up and went to the window to think. He needed antibiotics. It was such a simple fix but one that was impossible there. If she could get him to a modern-day doctor, she could save him. But how many times had she been to the cairn and failed to find the way through? It had worked for her only once. She shook her head helplessly. Apparently, she had to have her heart broken to get through it. She froze for a moment. *Or be in some sort of heightened emotional state.* All along, she'd been thinking it had something to do with the sun or the time of day, which might be the case. But what if it also had to do with emotions and the resulting energy? She exhaled with frustration. She was making no sense, even to herself. It didn't matter how or why the cairn worked. All that mattered was whether she could get him through it. All Rory needed was a doctor, and she knew where to find one.

When the captain left the room to send for the doctor, she pulled Angus aside. "I need you to trust me."

He shrugged. "Have I ever not?"

"You've never had need to, but I'm asking you now to listen to me."

His brow creased as he watched her intently.

"Do you remember when you were children and Rory told you he had gone through the fairy cairn?"

He thought for a moment then chuckled and nodded.

Lucy looked straight into his eyes. "You've got to believe me. Your brother's life depends upon it."

He shook his head. "Lucy, you're making no sense."

"I know." She took a deep breath and let it out as she lifted her eyes to his. "I came through the fairy cairn."

His suspicious smile made it clear that he didn't believe her.

She grabbed his arms. "I came through the fairy cairn from the future. I didn't mean to. Rory found me, and he brought me here."

He eyed her with disbelief.

"Rory told me he went to the future when he was a child."

"Lucy, I ken you're upset about Rory, but have you lost your mind?"

"No, but you'll lose your brother if we don't get him to a doctor."

"Father's sending someone to fetch him."

Frantic, Lucy shook her head. "Only a doctor from the future can save him."

Angus frowned but did not disagree or protest, so Lucy continued. "We need to get him to the fairy cairn. I don't know if it will work. I've been trying to get back myself. But if we don't try, he'll die."

Angus's frown was gone as he studied her. "You're in love with him."

"Yes."

"So you'd do him no harm."

"No." She peered at him with pleading eyes.

He leveled a frank look. "You ken you sound mad as a hatter."

"Yes."

Angus looked at the door to the hall. It was clear for the moment. He nodded. "All right."

"Angus, I could hug you!"

"I'd get in more trouble that way." He had already turned to get Rory. When they reached the door, they heard the captain upstairs, telling the butler to prepare a room for the doctor, who would likely be spending the night. They moved along close to the wall, hoping the afternoon shadows would mask their presence from anyone rounding the corner to come down the stairs. They heard the captain's voice at the top of the stairs as they pulled the door closed behind them.

Rory mumbled as they dragged him along to the stable. They placed Rory down on some hay, then Angus helped the groom and the stable boy hitch up a cart. They laid Rory in it with Lucy beside him, and Angus drove.

Having found Rory's room and the library empty, the captain came outside as they were riding away. He called after them, "Just what do you think you're doing?"

"Saving his life!" Lucy cried.

THE SUN CAST its last rays on the cairn as they arrived. "Just help me get him inside."

"But I'm coming with you," Angus said.

Lucy looked up. "No, you need to stay here. Effie needs you."

His brow furrowed, but he didn't refuse. "God's teeth!" A stunned Angus stared at the cairn.

Lucy turned to see light coming through from the other side. Rory moaned as Lucy hooked his arm over her shoulder and pulled him along. "C'mon, Rory, just a few steps." He was too tall and heavy, but she managed to stumble with him toward the light, then they fell.

CHAPTER 12
THE MEETING

L ucy looked up and saw strings of twinkling electric lights beyond the trees and the familiar lawn that sloped down to the Hudson River. It was the wedding venue.

"Rory! We've done it!"

He struggled to lift his head.

She found a leafy spot for him to lie down, then she tore part of her underskirt and tied it on a tree limb to mark the spot. "I'll be right back."

Lucy ran right into a bridal procession in her tartan gown, yelling, "Call an ambulance. I need a doctor! Someone's hurt!"

There was no doctor at the wedding, but one of the guests was a paramedic. While the wedding proceeded, the paramedic followed Lucy to Rory. "He's got an infection. He needs antibiotics."

"What happened to him?"

While they waited for the ambulance, the paramedic attended to Rory and managed to ask too many questions that Lucy couldn't answer. She rode with Rory to the hospital and watched them wheel him away. Then she sank into a waiting room chair and buried her face in her hands.

Every hour or so, someone came to give her an update. They were giving him strong IV antibiotics, but he'd been septic when he'd arrived, so they were cautious about his prognosis. When pointedly asked, they couldn't say whether he would pull through. Hour after hour, it was the same thing. At one point, they said he was stable. That was good, she supposed. But they were only cautiously optimistic.

A loud commotion woke Lucy from her slumber. How she'd managed to sleep in a hospital waiting room chair spoke to her exhaustion. She heard Rory's voice as nurses and orderlies rushed by. "I'll not be poked like a pincushion. God's wounds! What's this?"

"That's your catheter, hon," a nurse said.

Lucy followed the commotion and found Rory sitting up, ripping IVs out of his arm and swinging his legs over the side of the hospital bed as three orderlies struggled to restrain him.

"Rory! It's okay. Let them work on you. They're saving your life."

He stopped and looked at her as she stood in the doorway.

"You've been sick. Let them help you."

He gave her a questioning look, and she nodded. Everyone stared at her for an instant then proceeded to reconnect his IVs and equipment. A doctor ordered something that sent Rory back to sleep.

When they'd gotten him hooked up to his IVs again, a

nurse came to Lucy. "Would you like to sit in here with him?"

"Yes!"

The nurse smiled. "It's as much for us as for you. You've got a calming effect on him."

"How is he?"

She smiled. "The fact that he had the energy for all that is a good sign."

"He's not like that usually."

The nurse nodded. "It's the sepsis. Give the meds time to work."

Lucy was pretty sure he would have reacted the same way even if he'd awoken in a hospital room with a hangnail. Two IVs, monitors, and a urinary catheter would have been enough to send any eighteenth-century Highlander reaching for his sword. The nurse left, and Lucy sank into the chair beside Rory's bed.

She didn't know how long she'd dozed before a nurse woke her. They were moving Rory from the ER to a room. They were full of questions about his insurance coverage, but she told them he was visiting from out of the country, so she would have to get his travel insurance information after he woke. That bought her some time.

When Rory was settled in his room, Lucy picked up the phone by his bed and tried to call her mother but got her voice mail.

"Mom, it's me. I'm back. I'm with a sick friend in the hospital, and I was wondering if you could come by. I can't very well stay with Tyler, so I was hoping I might stay with you. I'm kind of stranded here, so do you think you could stop by Tyler's and bring me my purse? Make sure my phone's in it? And some jeans and a T-shirt?" She left the hospital name and number and hung up.

She had to get out of her tartan dress. People were starting to look at her strangely, or maybe she was only beginning to notice.

Six hours later, Lucy's mother hadn't called back. Since she'd retired a year earlier, Wendy Buchanan spent more time out of the country than in. God knew which elder hostel, or even which country, was housing her now.

Lucy was asleep with her head on her arms at the edge of Rory's hospital bed when the phone rang. She bolted upright and looked about for a couple of seconds before she recalled where she was, then she picked up the phone.

"Hi, honey! I just got your message."

"Mom." She was unexpectedly overwhelmed to hear her mother's voice, but she pulled it together. "Where are you?"

"I'm on safari."

"Of course you are. Why wasn't that my first guess?"

"I've been worried about you. Are you okay?"

"Yes, Mom, I'm fine. I just needed some time." Lucy felt that warm, comforting feeling she could only get from talking to her mother.

"Well, you could have let someone know where you were. That was freaky, seeing you walk through that cave. And then we looked everywhere and couldn't find you. Where did you go?"

"Long story."

"Oh, well, I had to borrow a sat phone. I probably shouldn't talk too long."

"Okay."

"Stay at my place. You know where the key is. I fly into Newark the day after tomorrow. See you then!"

"Okay, Mom. Mom?"

"Yes, honey?"

"I love you."

"I love you too. See you soon!" Her mother said it in that matter-of-fact tone she'd used since Lucy was a young child being put on the bus in the mornings.

"God's teeth," Rory grumbled. "I could use a wee dram."

Lucy glanced over to find Rory looking at her as if he hadn't been alternating between feverish delirium and unconsciousness for days. Lucy realized she had a death grip on Rory's hand, so she loosened her grasp. "Sorry." She looked around. "I can't get you a whisky, but I might be able to scare up some ice chips."

"Ice chips? If you cannae at least get me a tankard of ale, I've no use for you, woman."

Her head whipped back toward him. He was lucky he was grinning.

Lucy spent the next couple of days explaining all the strange things he was seeing. He was fascinated by the phone and the TV, taking turns with each item, touching buttons and watching what happened. Lucy walked in from a quick trip to the bathroom to find him on the phone, chatting with someone.

"Oh, aye. Well, I dinnae go this far from the castle as a rule, although I do ride into Inverness once or twice a year. Aye, on horseback. How else?" He listened for a moment. "I like your accent too. What am I wearing? Well, not much at the moment." He looked up at Lucy. "What a strange thing to ask."

"Yeah." She took the phone away from him and hung up. "Rory, you can't just call strangers. Some of them are, well, strange."

"She asked where I was from, so I told her Kildermoor Castle, and one thing led to another."

"Yeah, that's what I'm afraid of. Look, Rory, you can't just tell people you've got a castle in Scotland where you wear a kilt and ride horses and have crofters that farm your land and pay you rent. If one of the nurses hears you, they might extend your stay for a psychological evaluation."

"Is that bad?"

"For you, it would be."

One of the things about Rory she'd always admired was his willingness to listen to others. She would defy anyone she knew to find a twenty-first-century guy who could listen like that. "Just let me do most of the talking until you're checked out."

His eyes were twinkling.

"What?"

"You're quite bossy in the future." When he smiled at her like that, he could say pretty much anything, but she would never share that with him.

She handed him the TV remote. "Here, play with this for a while."

He set down the remote and took hold of her hand. "I could, but this is far more interesting." He pressed his lips to her hand.

Lucy grinned. "Somebody's feeling better." She practically giggled, but her smile faded quickly when she looked up at the doorway.

"Tyler." She recovered from her momentary shock as he handed her a grocery bag.

His expression looked like a cross between sheepish and a deer in headlights. For some reason, animal similes were all she could manage for Tyler.

He stared at her as if she were a ghost, which she was, in a way. "Your mom called me. Her flight was delayed."

"Oh. I wish that she hadn't bothered you with this."

He shrugged. "We looked all over for you after you disappeared through that cave."

"Yeah, pretty much." That worked as well as any explanation she could think of. There was no use trying to fill in more credible details.

Tyler glanced toward Rory then continued, "Your history major-barista friend—"

"Brittney."

"Yeah, Brittney. Turns out she wrote a college paper on slavery in New York. Short version—not the version she shared with us, by the way—she was convinced you'd found an old runaway slave tunnel that led down to the river."

Lucy's brow furrowed as she listened with interest, then she nodded. "Uh, yeah, that's more or less how it went." She shrugged. "I needed some me time."

He looked down and nodded. A moment of awkwardness passed, then he gestured toward the shopping bag. "So... purse, phone, and charger, and some cash. Your car's downstairs in the lot. Parking lot ticket is in there too."

"Thanks. I'm sorry about this."

He nodded. "You okay?"

"Yeah, I am." As she said it, she realized how completely all right she was. At the same time, she thought she detected a tinge of sadness in Tyler's eyes.

"I'm Rory Munro." With a frosty smile, Rory bowed his head slightly and regarded Tyler with what must have been the eighteenth-century version of a laser death ray.

Lucy's mouth hung open for a moment. "Oh, sorry. Tyler, this is—"

"Rory. We've met." Tyler looked as though he had a right to object to Rory's presence but remembered he didn't. "And Rory is..."

"My boyfriend." She nervously blurted it out, and now there was no turning back as the words spilled forth. "Yeah, we met in Scotland."

Tyler nodded, looking confused. "Scotland?"

She flipped her hair. She never flipped her hair. "Yeah, I just went there," she said with an uneasy laugh. "Oh yeah, Rory has a castle there. His father's the laird. When he's not here with me, he wears kilts and rides horses. He taught me to ride. We go riding a lot. On the glen. That's a valley, and—"

"Lucy," Rory interrupted. He smiled graciously, but his brow was a tiny bit creased. "Would you mind checking to see if the nurse has my ice chips?"

Lucy squinted, but Rory just smiled back and raised his eyebrows.

"Uh, sure. C'mon, Tyler, I'll walk you to the elevator."

They endured awkward small talk while they waited. He told her she could come by anytime to get her belongings. She still had a key. She said she would call first and probably go on a weekday so she wouldn't bother him, by which she meant so she wouldn't have to see him again.

She exhaled in relief when the elevator door closed between them. Seeing Tyler for the first time since the wedding had been awkward and painful, but most of all, it had been a relief. She was glad that was done.

And they were done.

CHAPTER 13
A HISTORY LESSON

After a week in the hospital, Rory was ready to be anywhere else. Lucy had tried to prepare him for car travel, but nothing had prepared her for Rory's reaction. For the first several minutes, he hung his head out of the window to feel the wind on his face. Lucy wasn't sure what she'd expected, but it was clear she had an adrenaline junkie on her hands. Just watching him made her grin. Nothing fazed him. When he wasn't asking her to go faster, he was busy asking how —about everything.

"Ignition? You set it on fire?"

"Uh, well, I don't know. It's got spark plugs, so I guess there must be a spark somewhere."

"Why are flames not shooting out from the front there?"

"From the hood? Good question. I don't know."

After several more questions, Lucy pulled over to the side of the road and turned to him.

"Rory. It's a car. I don't know how it works, but it

works. When it doesn't, I take it to someone who knows how to make it work again. Honestly, it could be magic for all I know."

He drew back, alarmed. "Magic?"

"No! I didn't mean literally." Lucy reminded herself that in Rory's century, they'd only recently stopped burning witches in Scotland, so magic might not have been the best word to throw around lightly. "What I mean is, I don't know what goes on under the hood. All I've ever bothered to know was how to put this key in this ignition and drive."

"May I try?"

"Now? I don't know."

"I taught you to ride horses." He looked at her as if she owed him.

The look of triumph on his face told her there was no winning this one. "Well, okay, but not here on a winding mountain road. Tomorrow, I'll take you to an empty parking lot."

Lucy felt a sudden surge of compassion for every parent who'd ever taught a teenager to drive.

Rory leaned over to hug her but was stopped by the seat belt. "Och! Curse this harness you've forced me to wear!"

She did feel some sympathy but not as much as she'd felt for him the first time he put on briefs and blue jeans. He did not enjoy them at all. But she did. She smiled as she recalled her first glimpse of him walking about in his new clothes. Nope, she had no problem with Rory in jeans.

They pulled into the driveway at her mother's house. "Is your mother a crofter?"

"No, many of us live in small houses these days. Although there are some of what you would call castles down the road in Westchester County."

After they got out of the car, Lucy opened the fake rock her mom kept near the porch and pulled the house key out. "It's not a real rock," she explained before Rory could ask. "It's supposed to trick burglars."

"But can they not just use it to break the glass?"

"I guess they could, but no one has yet." She opened the front door. "My mother's a crazy adventurer. She's away more than she's home."

Once they'd set down their shopping bags, Lucy took Rory's hand and led him out to the deck. Built high on a hill, the house overlooked a reservoir. Because it was one of many that supplied drinking water to New York City, homes were not built near the shore, leaving an unspoiled view of woodlands and shimmering water.

Lucy leaned her elbows on the deck rail. "Do you like it here?"

"Oh, aye." Rory turned from the view and fixed his eyes on Lucy. "'Tis a fine view wherever I look." He stepped closely behind her, pulled her into his arms, and looked out at the view.

"I mean here in this century," Lucy said.

"Aye, I like it just fine."

She gazed out over the reservoir. "I'm sorry I took you away from your home. I know you must miss your family and castle."

"You saved my life."

"But you saw what I went through when I tried to come home. What if you can't go back?"

"My family's there and my home and land that I love."

Lucy looked down and nodded. Rory gave her shoulders a squeeze. "But the woman I love is right here."

"I don't have a castle or even a home. And I lost my job while I was away. I can't promise you much."

"Then just promise me you."

She would have answered if he hadn't kissed her.

AFTER THEIR PARKING lot driving lesson the next morning, Rory rested his hands on the wheel of Lucy's parked car, looking deeply disappointed. "A learner's permit?"

Lucy winced. "Yeah, I probably shouldn't have let you do this much."

"Then let us go get a permit."

She wrinkled her face. "I don't think we can. You haven't got any ID. Identification. You're kind of an illegal alien where the law is concerned." She sighed. "When we get home, I can look it up to be sure."

"I didnae see a library at your mother's house."

"No, but we've got something better—the internet." She answered his questioning look. "Just wait."

"IT'S ANOTHER TV." Rory stood beside Lucy as she sat at her desk.

"Hold on." She opened a browser window and began to type. As she clicked on results, Rory moved closer and leaned on the desk.

As she had suspected, Rory's learner's permit was not

going to happen. But by the time she was sure, Rory had discovered the wondrous power of internet links.

"I can look up anything?" he asked.

She nodded. "Pretty much."

"May I?"

She smiled and handed him the wireless keyboard. Rory proceeded to hunt and peck his way through "Kildermoor Castle." When a page of search results appeared, he leaned back in surprise.

Lucy watched his joy quickly turn to dismay.

HE READ the web page with a sinking gut feeling, then he read it again. "Is this real? Could there be some mistake?"

Lucy's wide-open eyes did not ease his fears. "Well, it's the internet. Not everything on it is true." She switched places with him and began typing search terms and opening windows. One after another confirmed the news until he put his hand over her typing fingers. "That's enough." He stood and went out to the deck. Lucy followed, but when he held out his palm without turning, she left him alone.

The text remained on the monitor: "The once grand Kildermoor Castle was lost late one evening in a high-stakes faro card game, rendering the new laird and his father homeless."

One sentence on a history website had dispensed with Rory's home and the life he had known. He sank into a chair and silently wept. Lest Lucy see him unman himself, he tamped it all down and regained his composure as well as he could. Then he thought of those heather-clad braes that sloped down, and the burn that flowed through the glen. How he used to love walking through the knee-deep heather up to the place where the mist touched the mountains. It was all lost—his home and everything in it.

And Angus. Laird?

The internet said it had happened in 1746, but it didn't say on what date. What if there was a chance he could prevent it?

He had to go back.

LUCY LEANED against the kitchen counter and watched Rory on the deck. He'd waved her away. Now he sat in a chair, his face buried in his hands.

She could only imagine how devastating it must have been for him to read what had happened. He was too proud to be seen in a moment of weakness, assuming it could be called weak to be vulnerable. But he came from a time and a place where men's idea of fun competition was to throw giant logs and stones. Winning was not so much about beating another man down as it was showing superior strength. Conversely, losing came not from defeat at the hands of another, but from one's own lesser strength. Strength was power.

To be seen in a moment of powerlessness would be more than any proud Highlander could bear. But she wondered if men in his century had ever considered the strength of the women beside them. Theirs was a silent strength not built upon flashy displays of power, but from compassion tempered by well-reasoned thought and unwavering constancy. Lucy wanted to be that for him, but she stood on the threshold, unable to take that one last step to be with him whatever may come and, at the heart of the matter, wherever.

When she could stand it no more, she slid open the glass door and went out to Rory. He reached out his hand and pulled her onto his lap, then he held her for a long while, with only the gentle whispers of leaves interrupting the quiet.

"I must go back."

"I know."

To say she was torn did no justice to the torment she felt as she prepared to leave her home forever. She only hoped that she could follow through and go with him. Yet deep in her heart, she could not see herself walking away from her life.

When she was growing up, she and her mother had always been a team, and their team had won life. Her mother had shown her that a woman's strength did not come from a man, but from within. She'd taught Lucy to strive and to work hard toward her goals, and Lucy was beginning to achieve her life goals. Her career was going well. She had a small nest egg. She had good friends. The truth was, she wanted for nothing—at least, that was what she'd thought before she met Rory.

Rory had toppled the foundation she'd thought her life was built upon. He was the polar opposite of Tyler, a man she'd been with for many years. Yet one month with Rory had made her forget about the years spent with Tyler. Rory had a fiery passion for life, his home, and his family that shone through his eyes and drove everything he did.

Lucy had never felt that kind of passion for her job or

her life, so to be near someone like that was a thrill. And that was the problem. Was her time with Rory like a vacation fling in which everything seemed magical because it wasn't real even though she pretended that it was? Or were her feelings enough to give up everything? Everything. Forever.

She wasn't quite sure, and Rory hadn't specifically asked her if she was coming with him. He either assumed it or hoped it, unwilling to upset the delicate balance of logic from which she would base her decision.

Because she couldn't decide, she put it off. It only made sense to get her things in order. That way, her options were open. To that end, she wrote a letter to her mother, explaining everything, including the location of the stone chamber in case something went wrong. What that could be, she didn't know, but it seemed like the smart thing to do. The only things left were her personal belongings, her bank account, and her 401K. She hadn't changed banks since her college days, so her mother was still an authorized signer on her checking and savings. Her mom could transfer what was left before she declared Lucy missing. As the designated beneficiary of her 401K, her mother would receive its funds after Lucy was declared dead. That took her breath for a moment. Her mother would have to go through that.

Clothed in his plaid and drinking a craft beer, Rory stopped pacing the deck and peeked inside. "Lucy, the sun will set soon."

"Ready." Lucy wiped her eyes and picked up her backpack containing her eighteenth-century garb, and they were off.

RATHER THAN TROMP across the grounds of the wedding venue, they hiked through the woods and arrived at the stone chamber well before dark. Rory stooped to look inside then came back out. There was no need for Lucy to look to determine the state of the stone chamber, but she did.

She spoke as though sounding sensible would make it happen. "We'll keep trying."

In Rory's eyes, Lucy saw the same crestfallen look he must have seen so many times back in Scotland. Abstracted, he nodded.

Overwhelming relief washed over her, and she felt guilty for it. Yes, she wanted what was best for him. But if that was not possible, she wanted him. If the chamber didn't work, that meant she would not have to choose. She slipped her arms about his waist and laid her head against his chest. He held her and accepted her comfort, not knowing that his torment had brought her relief.

Leaves crunched, and twigs snapped as someone approached.

"Oh, thank God I'm not too late!"

"Mom?"

There stood Wendy Buchanan, a fit forty-something brunette with a short, wavy bob, wearing a tank shirt, cargo pants, and hiking shoes. Lucy rushed into her arms.

"I was so scared I'd missed you." Wendy stepped back and held Lucy's face in her hands. "I read your letter. Oh my gosh, Lucy!" She hugged her again. There were tears in her eyes. "I'm so happy to see you."

Lucy took her mom's hand and turned. "This is Rory."

After a knowing smile, Wendy gave Rory a hug.

Seeing the slightly stunned look on Rory's face, Lucy explained, "We hug a lot here in the future—or at least in my family." She grinned broadly.

Wendy glanced at the stone chamber then at Lucy. "So what happens now?"

"I don't know." Lucy's gaze drifted from her mother to Rory. "Should we wait?"

Rory nodded grimly then glanced inside the chamber.

Lucy and Wendy were busily catching up on Lucy's adventure and Wendy's trip home, when Rory said, "Lucy."

Not hearing him, Wendy continued. "And then the baboon stole my purse—with my cell phone and passport!"

"Lucy," Rory said a bit more insistently. "Look."

Sunlight poured in through the back of the chamber.

Out of sheer ingrained politeness, Rory gave Wendy his full attention long enough to say, "Mrs. Buchanan, it's been a pleasure to meet you."

Lucy stared at her mother then at Rory.

A helpless expression crossed Rory's face as he held out his hand. "We need to go."

All she seemed able to do was look into his eyes, those dark, deep-set eyes that she loved.

"Lucy?"

Slowly, she shook her head.

Rory took her into his arms. "Don't do this. You know I can't stay. My family needs me."

"Mine too. I'm sorry."

He stood there, unwilling to leave yet unable to stay.

A thick mist covered the opening as it started to fade. With a look so bereft that her heart broke, he said, "I will always love you." He kissed her fiercely then tore himself away and walked into the stone chamber.

Wendy gripped Lucy's shoulders. "Go after him."

"I can't leave... here."

Wendy looked shocked. "You mean me. Listen to me. Do you love him?"

"Yes."

"Then you're going." She spoke with a mother's insistence, but Lucy couldn't seem to move.

Then Wendy's eyes brightened, and she lifted her chin. "You know, I haven't been to Scotland in ages." With that, Wendy pushed Lucy into the stone chamber and through the fading stone wall.

CHAPTER 14

TRAVELS WITH WENDY

"Wow!" Wendy dusted off her cargo pants and looked back at the solid wall of stones she'd just come through. "That was insane!" She was practically slack-jawed as she surveyed the rich green hills that surrounded them.

"Mom! What have you done?"

Wendy smiled. "Moved to Scotland?"

Lucy hugged her mother then turned to Rory, who swept her into a desperate embrace. "We'll make a good life here, I promise."

She touched her fingertips to his lips. "We're together. That's all I care about."

Wendy looked around at the dramatic Highland landscape. "Nice place you've got here, Rory."

"Wendy? Are you all right?"

Wendy shrugged. "I'm fine. It was this one who thought she should sacrifice her own happiness for my sake, which was sweet but not the best choice by far." She put an arm about Lucy's shoulder. "Sorry to invite myself like this, but you know how I love to travel."

Lucy was still in a state of disbelief. "But Mom..."

Wendy grinned. "Is eighteenth-century Scotch as good as in our time? Why don't we go to that inn over there and do a sampler?"

"Not in those clothes, you don't, madam." Rory glanced sideways at Wendy's cargo pants. "Lucy, can you give her one of your underskirts? I'll go see about borrowing some horses to get us back home." He stopped. "I'm not sure where that is."

They had never been able to find a record of the exact date of the card game when the estate was lost. Rory thought for a moment. "I'll go in to the inn and ask to borrow some horses. I'll mention that I've been away. If anything's happened, they'll tell me soon enough. Lucy, change your dress and wait outside the inn where someone can see you. That way, they won't question my wanting two horses."

"We'll just go around here and change, then." The two women walked around to the opposite side of the cairn while Rory waited. Lucy smiled at his discomfort over the immodesty of the whole situation. They emerged with Lucy wearing the tartan dress she'd gone home in, and Wendy in one of her underskirts topped by her soft-shell jacket. With the women properly clothed, Rory felt it safe to leave them to go into the inn.

He returned minutes later more slowly than he'd gone in. When he reached Lucy, he took her hand and continued to walk without missing a step. "We're too late. He lost the estate five days ago. I was still in the hospital then." Rory frowned but walked on without speaking.

"Oh." She was almost as disappointed as he was, but what was there to say? It hurt to see him agonizing over an impossible situation, but she was powerless to offer help or comfort.

"There was nothing you could have done, you know. If you'd stayed here, you wouldn't have lived to prevent it."

He glanced in her direction. "Aye. Maybe that's what bothers me most. There was nothing anyone could have done—except Angus. It was all up to him. He had to ken how many people depended upon him. It's not only our family. Dozens of servants and workers, as well as their families, depended upon us. With any luck, the new owner will keep the existing staff, but he might be moving his entire household here. Either way, everyone who lived on the estate will be affected by this to some degree. And it didnae have to happen." He shook his head and took a deep breath. "Well, we're here now, so it's best to look forward."

Wendy, although sympathetic, was in her element, invigorated by the crisp Highland air, rambling through parts unknown. Lucy couldn't help but smile. This was quintessential Wendy. Nothing fazed her. She just changed clothes and fell into step.

Still, Lucy wondered. "Mom, why did you do it?"

"Do what, honey?"

"I mean, I'm happy to have you here—thrilled, actually. But you just walked away from your whole life on a whim."

Wendy gave Lucy one of those over-the-glasses looks, except she didn't wear glasses. "You, my dear, are hardly a whim. You're my life. And although I was moved by your willingness to stay, I couldn't watch you give up the love of your life."

Lucy lowered her voice. "Mom, I don't know that he's that. I've only known him for a little over a month. How can you just know something like that?"

Wendy stopped. "If I can tell by looking at you, then you already know. You're just afraid to admit it."

"Because it doesn't make sense. There's no such thing as love at first sight. Tyler and I were together for years before we even thought about marriage."

"And look how well that turned out," Wendy muttered under her breath before looking up at Lucy. "Nobody said love makes sense."

Lucy's troubled expression said it all. Wendy smiled and walked on, looking satisfied to have confirmation for what she already knew. "So to answer your question, I did not walk away from my life on a whim. I walked toward it. And now we begin a new adventure." She slipped her arm into Lucy's.

Lucy couldn't help but tear up a bit. There was no mom like her mom. "But you know this isn't like going on safari. There's no guarantee you can ever go back."

"Don't worry about me. I can take care of myself."

And she had. Wendy had been there every step of the way until it was time for Lucy to go off to college and build her own life. Her mom had then spent a decade traveling about with no discernible path or agenda in mind, finally able to live her own life, independent of responsibility for Lucy. Maybe that was why it troubled Lucy to see her give up that life once more for her daughter. For selfish reasons, Lucy was glad it had worked out that way. She only hoped it would work out as well for her mother.

They resumed walking with Rory, who had been silent for most of the way, speaking only of practical matters like water and food. For some reason, he had neglected to offer whether he'd found out any more at the inn. Lucy trusted he would tell her when he was ready.

Unfortunately, her patience wasn't as enduring as her trust. "Umm, Rory, exactly where are we going?"

He swallowed. "My father and brother took what personal belongings they could in a cart and moved out days ago."

"To where?" Lucy tried not to sound frustrated, but she had never been good at being left in the dark.

Rory ran his fingers through his shock of dark hair. "They had nowhere to go, so Effie took them in. They're living in a croft."

Now Lucy was almost as stunned as Rory but for different reasons, perhaps. Under the circumstances, Effie had done a selfless and generous thing.

"Who's Effie?" Wendy asked.

"Long story, Mom. I'll fill you in later."

"She felt sorry for them." Rory looked at Lucy, still not believing. "After what Angus did, she still had enough pity to take them into her home."

Lucy stared at the hills in the distance. "She's a kind soul."

"Aye."

"It must have horrified her when her father shot you. Maybe this is her way of making it up to you."

Wendy turned and stared. "Shot you?"

Rory chimed in with Lucy, "Long story."

"Long walk," Wendy countered.

So Lucy filled her in.

WENDY TURNED out to be in better shape than Lucy, who had spent far too much quality time in the cubicle farm at work. She kept up with her companions but not with the apparent ease they enjoyed, so the sight of Effie's croft at midday brought her joy.

Rory called out, and Effie rushed out of the croft, followed by Angus and the captain. After a joyous reunion, the captain met Wendy's eyes and bowed.

"Captain, I'd like you to meet my mother, Wendy Buchanan."

Wendy held out her hand to shake his, but he kissed hers instead.

Lucy's brow creased. Was her mother... No. What? She was not blushing. She slipped her arm inside her mother's and drew Wendy's attention away. "This is Rory's brother, Angus." *Angus, the man who single-handedly destroyed the family legacy. That Angus.*

Effie invited them all inside, where a peat fire in the center of the room warmed the croft and sent ribbons of smoke to the soot-blackened roof while sunlight made a feeble attempt to enter through the two closed windows. Rory took Effie's hand and held it in both of his. Deep emotion lined his forehead. "What you've done is far more than we deserve."

She met his gaze. "Och, Mr. Rory—"

"Just Rory." He looked at her sternly.

"Rory," she said uncomfortably.

"I ken that a thank-you doesnae pay the fiddler, but I thank you nonetheless."

She shook her head, smiling. "I'll wager you're thirsty. I'll get you some ale."

Lucy looked about the inside of the croft and took a silent count. Two box beds in the corner, six people, and a cow. There were barely enough places to sit, and that was only because two of them sat on the edge of the box beds. This was bound to be interesting.

The captain spent the afternoon fishing and returned with two salmon for supper. To that, Effie added some turnips and kale from the garden. It was a good meal, but the mood was subdued, for no one had yet mentioned the cause for their presence at Effie's. Rory was polite but barely looked at his brother. The captain was exceedingly courteous to Effie, clearly mindful that she was the reason they had a roof overhead at all. Lucy made eye contact with Effie a couple of times, enough to know there were things they would talk about later. So went the reunion.

Lucy and her mother shared a box bed, which left the other for Effie. The three men slept on the floor by the fire, and the cow had a stall on the opposite side of the croft. Lucy drifted to sleep, hoping the scent of the peat fire might overpower that of the cow. To her misfortune, the peat wasn't up to the task.

She awoke the next morning to find Effie coming into the croft with a basket of eggs, which she set on a table not far from the fire. Lucy got up as Effie whipped up a batch of bannocks, which she cooked on the griddle, followed by the eggs. The table was too small for six people, so they sat where they could and held plates on their laps.

Lucy watched the Munro men and wondered how this must be for them. She and her mother had lived a relatively simple life, and this was hardly different from the camping trips they used to go on together. But these men had grown up knowing nothing but luxury. Croft life must have been a hard landing for them.

CHAPTER 15
THE PRICE OF LOSING

The first order of business was to build a shed for the cow. Rory correctly guessed that the women—and the men, truth be told—might prefer a different arrangement. The men gathered stones and constructed back and side walls at the end of the croft, while the women gathered heather to make a thatched roof.

On one of their many stone-gathering expeditions, Rory found a moment alone with his father. "What happened?"

"There's not much to tell. Your brother gambled and lost."

There was no proper way to ask his next question without risking offense. "How was the estate in his possession to lose?"

They walked for several more steps in silence before Captain Munro answered him. "I made an error in judgment." He glanced at Rory and continued. "When you left, Angus took over running the estate, as you had been so ably doing. He'd dabbled in it before, but I didnae ken whether he knew how to manage an estate of that size. I wanted to train him, to prepare him to take over when I was gone, as I had with you."

That, as Rory recalled, had happened by default when the captain had given up on Angus and turned to Rory out of necessity.

"I watched him manage the day-to-day affairs of the estate, advising when needed," the captain said. "He'd always had an aptitude for figures. He was too charming by half in his dealing with people. I suppose that stood him well in his gambling too. Something changed. Whether it was your getting shot and then leaving or his, well, indiscretion with Effie, he seemed to be taking life more seriously. He stopped playing cards, and I started to believe in him again. I knew if he'd only set his mind to something, he could excel. And he did.

"Maybe what he'd needed all along was responsibility. Now he had it. Except for a family. Family changes a man. It makes him live for someone beyond himself or his own needs. If Angus were married, he'd want to be strong and honorable for the sake of his wife and his children." The captain looked Rory in the eye. "Maybe it would keep him out of trouble."

What could Rory have said? He agreed because that was the sympathetic thing to do, but the notion was mad from its inception. Angus had stopped gambling because that was what he did periodically. But he would always go back. It was a pattern that had gone on for years, but the captain was too blinded by love for his firstborn to see it.

The two unloaded the barrow of rocks by the croft.

Angus continued building the stone wall, while Rory and his father headed back to the fields for more.

The captain continued. "So I set about finding Angus a wife. Of course, Effie was unsuitable, but I thought I could find someone willing. After all, he stood to inherit Kildermoor, an impressive estate by any man's measure. But I'd underestimated Angus's reputation. The fact that he'd attempted to deflower, and I suspect succeeded in a number of cases, enough eligible ladies—when word got around, the fathers of those left were unwilling to chance it. Not that his philandering alone would have been a deterrent, but with it came the high-stakes gaming. They wouldn't send their daughters to a life that might land them, well, here."

Rory frowned and stared into the distance. "So you deeded everything to him..."

"To make him worth taking a risk. With his wealth and estate, who could resist?"

Apparently not Angus. Rory didn't need to hear any more. As soon as the ink was dry on his father's signature, Angus couldn't pass up the chance to go out and enjoy his good fortune. Rory supposed it didn't matter whom his brother had lost to. Word must have gotten out that Angus had serious funds to play with. He'd been a mark visible from miles around. It had only been a matter of time, which in Angus's case, turned out to be days.

While the men built the stone wall, Effie taught the women to make rope from heather they'd gathered from the moor. Lucy and her mother collected it in their gathered-up skirts, while Effie carried the bulk in a basket slung over her shoulders. By the end of a week, the men had added a roof roughly framed from cut branches and covered in thatch held together by the heather rope the women had made. When they'd finished, they led the cow inside its new home and admired their work as the last of the sun lit the tops of the mountains.

Lucy shivered. Rory drew closer and wrapped part of his plaid around her. As he did, he leaned over and whispered, "We've not had a moment alone, and I miss you."

Lucy didn't reply. She just looked into his eyes and then looked away, smiling.

As they all went into the cottage, the captain said, "This calls for a celebration." He opened his portmanteau and pulled out a bottle of whisky. "I took the liberty of pilfering this from the castle for a special occasion. I think we're all thirsty enough to consider this occasion special enough."

They all agreed and sat down to enjoy some rest and a wee dram or two.

Several drams later, Wendy, Effie, and the captain were staring into the fire and taking turns singing ballads. Rory touched Lucy's arm and tilted his head toward the door. He got up and took Lucy's hand, drawing her to her feet. The singers turned toward them, still singing.

"Just going out for some air." Ignoring a teasing glance or two, Rory grabbed a blanket on the way outside.

With the door closed behind them, he wrapped the blanket around Lucy and pulled her into his arms and planted a long kiss. "I've been wanting to do that all day."

The moon wasn't quite full, but it cast enough light for Lucy to see Rory's head angled down to gaze at her.

"Are you sure that you've done the right thing—coming back here with me?" Rory asked.

"Yes. I hesitated because I was worried about leaving

my mother behind. As you know, every trip through that stone chamber could be the last, but she basically forced me."

Rory crinkled his brow. "That doesn't bode well for me."

Lucy grinned and shook her head. "Do you know what she said?"

"That you put up a good fight?"

She laughed. "No. My mother said she did it because you're the one."

He suppressed a satisfied smile. "Was she right?"

"Yes," Lucy said without hesitation.

"Then say it." He took her face in his hands and brushed his lips against hers. "I love you so. Tell me you feel the same way."

"Yes," she said softly.

He pressed fervent lips to hers then whispered, "Say the words."

"I love you."

They kissed, and neither cared how cold the night air was.

Rory kissed her forehead and hair. "It's selfish of me to want you here. You've given up so much, and I've nothing to offer."

"You. That's all I want." Lucy looked into Rory's eyes then sank back into his arms.

"But lass, there's no TV here."

Her eyes lit with amusement. "I'm not saying I haven't made sacrifices, but you're worth it."

They laughed, and he lifted and swung her about. "Lucy Buchanan, you're more wondrous than a TV remote or even a cell phone."

"Rory, think what you're saying."

"You're right, lass. The cold air has made me daft. We'd best go back inside." But when she turned to leave, he pulled her back into his arms. He spoke in a low voice as he kissed his way down her neck. "Bonnie Lucy, you're driving me daft. It's all I can do to look at you and not lift you up into my arms and carry you off." He pressed his body against her and kissed her again.

"And where would you carry me off to?" she whispered.

"Och, I dinnae think I could carry you past the bed."

She wrinkled her face. "Thanks?"

"Oh, I could carry you farther, I just wouldnae want to." He brushed his lips against hers. "Do you ken how I want you?"

"Yes," she whispered as she tightened her arms about him and kissed him.

WHEN THEY FINALLY CAME IN from the cold, they found Wendy teaching the others a Joni Mitchell song. Despite all the pieces of Lucy's life that didn't quite fit together, that moment felt right. All her family and friends were together and singing. That was where they all belonged.

Except Angus. Angus sat quietly off to the side. He hadn't been himself since they'd arrived. But from Lucy's perspective, he'd earned every tormenting pang of guilt and remorse he suffered, so she'd left him to suffer alone. But now, as he sat there alone and aloof, she saw only a man who was broken. She could not believe he had ever set out to do anyone harm. He was a victim of his own character. He was a rake. He was selfish and thoughtless. Perhaps worst of all was what he'd done to Effie, whose only weakness had been her naïve trust. He had allowed her to care when he'd known that he didn't. In doing so, he had broken something fragile, which although repaired, would not be the same.

RORY AND ANGUS stood on the banks of the river, determined to catch enough salmon for supper. The walk there had been quiet, which was typical for Angus these days.

"What happened, Angus?"

"I think the answer to that is painfully obvious."

"Not to me. Why did you not stop?"

Angus clenched his jaw as he stared at the swiftly flowing river before him. "Do you not think I've asked myself that dozens—hundreds—of times? It all seems so simple unless you're the one there."

"But I wasn't because I wouldn't have been."

Angus turned burning eyes to his brother. He could barely get out the words. "I couldnae stop."

Rory watched his brother crumble into a heap of emotion that he'd never displayed. Angus wept. The most heartbreaking aspect of it was the hopeless effort he expended to try to conceal it. Rory gripped Angus's shoulder.

When Angus had pulled himself together enough to speak, he said, "I ken well that you wouldnae understand.

You're the fine, noble Rory, upon whom everyone can rely."

Rory winced but held his tongue.

Self-loathing darkened Angus's expression. "Do you not think it's hurt all these years to see how everyone discounts me? From earliest I can remember, I've always been the one getting into mischief. I didn't set out to do it. It just happened. People came to expect it, and I did not disappoint. But I failed with such charm that the only one truly disappointed was I. Even then, what did it matter, really? I was the heir."

Rory spoke quietly. "But you left me to pick up the pieces. Every mess you ever made, I cleaned up."

Angus turned to Rory in disbelief. "Because that's what you do. Every time."

Rory grimaced, wanted to protest, yet he could not deny it was true.

Angus looked at Rory with the peace of one long since resigned to his fate. "You cannae stop making everything right any more than I can stop making it wrong."

Rory stared as the water rushed by and the salmon leaped into the air, landing ahead of a current that would only sweep them backward. Yet they did it again and again. Into the rushing current they swam because it had always been so.

The brothers continued to fish, content with the sound of the water and the breeze that stirred the trees and sent leaves fluttering downward.

Angus broke the silence. "It was different this time." He said it as though there hadn't been a long silence since either had spoken.

"Different?" Torn from his own thoughts, Rory wasn't quite sure to what Angus was referring.

"I've lost before, and I've seen others lose. But I've never seen anyone win like this friend of the Baron of Swordale's. In truth, had Swordale not vouched for his character, I'd have been sure he was cheating."

Rory was skeptical. "Because he won?"

"Aye, but it's how he won. Swordale held the bank, while his friend, Mr. Skeates, played and won almost every turn. And when he didnae win, the bank did. There were more than a handful of players, each one of us losing. As long as I've been playing the game, I've never seen anything like it. It was unnatural. So I began to study the baron and his friend, Mr. Skeates. They never looked at one another. Ever. Each time Swordale drew a card, for a split second before he drew it, he would react. It was as if he knew what it was going to be. But I couldn't figure out how."

"How can you be sure he was cheating?"

Angus looked Rory straight in the eye. "I know I've made quite a mess of my life, but in the process, I've seen a lot of card games and even more gamblers. I know all the types, how they win and how they lose. And how this gambler won didnae feel right."

Rory made no effort to hide his doubt.

"I ken what you're thinking, that I'm making excuses. But I accept responsibility for what happened. Who knows? It might have happened, anyway. If not at this game, then at another. But it happened at this game, and it happened with those men. And I'm sure they were cheating."

"If you suspected as much, then why did you continue to play?"

"I dinnae ken. I suppose, at the time, I didnae want to believe it. Our families have been friends since I can remember. I couldnae believe he would take everything from me, so I talked myself out of my suspicions, and I relied on my luck."

"But you're smarter than that."

Angus looked at his brother. "Am I?" He smiled to himself. "There, you see? We all choose to believe what we want to believe."

As they packed up and walked home, Rory brooded. Maybe Angus was right. But what good was knowing that now? When they were nearly home, Rory said, "They shouldnae be able to go about stealing from people."

"Who can stop them without proof? I'd have made myself look like less of a man for not losing with grace."

"We'll just have to find proof, then."

"Rory, cheating's a serious charge. You've not only got to be certain, but you've got to make everyone else certain as well. What's done is done. I dinnae blame you for hating me. I've disgraced our family, and I know it. But I am sorry."

"I cannae lie," Rory said. "It was a terrible shock and disappointment. I loved our home and every tree, burn, brae, and glen. But you are my brother, and you're more to me than all of it. So we'll find a way through. In the meanwhile, we've a place to stay and good people around us. Perhaps letting go of one treasure has made room for another."

"If you can find any treasure in this, then you're daft."

Rory looked ahead, deep in thought. "Maybe I am."

CHAPTER 16
FOR PEAT'S SAKE

L ucy and Wendy forced Effie to sit and relax while they washed the supper dishes. Everyone else was gathered in what had become his or her usual seat near the peat fire. As Lucy and Wendy finished the last of the dishes, Angus stood. "I have something to say."

Speech usually came easily to Angus, but he stammered. "I, well, I ken what a hardship... I ken that I've burdened your lives. Father"—he glanced at the captain but looked quickly away and swallowed back his emotions —"if it helps, I'll not ever forgive myself, so I wouldnae blame any of you for doing likewise."

Lucy had been hard on Angus, in thought if not in deed. To see him humbled like this was something she'd never expected to see, and it moved her.

Angus continued. "So I ask nothing of anyone. I just want you to ken that I'm sorry."

The captain gave a slight nod to Angus, while Rory

lifted his glass. "May the roof above never fall in, and may we below never fall out."

Angus met Rory's eyes, and something passed between them in the shorthand of siblings, while their father looked on. Wendy slipped her hand into Lucy's and gave it a squeeze, for they both knew the power of family, and this one had grown stronger.

THEIR DAYS WERE FILLED with preparing for winter. They dug peat and left it to dry in the sun. A week later, they went to load the dried peat bricks in baskets Effie called creels.

"Should you be doing this in your condition?" Wendy asked.

Effie hoisted a creel to her back. "Oh, I'm fine. I'm through with the sickness, but I promise I'll slow down when I'm as large as this basket." She grinned and kept on walking and knitting.

"I promise you will too," Wendy said. They all laughed.

As Lucy struggled to walk with a heavy creel on her back, she asked Effie, "Has anyone ever thought of putting wheels on these things?"

Effie laughed. "No, I dinnae think so. Not with this rough ground."

Wendy struggled alongside her daughter. "Do you think your spinner luggage could manage this dirt path?"

"Don't think I wouldn't try if I had it here." Lucy hoisted her basket back up from where it had slipped off her shoulder and was working its way to her neck. "What about choking? How many times a day does that happen?"

Effie laughed and called back, "Just keep it balanced across your shoulders, and you'll be fine."

Lucy trudged onward. "Sure, I will."

As they approached the road, a term used very loosely in Lucy's opinion, a carriage drove past. Effie watched it disappear around a bend. "Oh, that must be him. I didnae want to say anything to the captain and the Misters Munro, but I hear Mr. Skeates is moving in to the castle."

By the time they reached home, the Munro men had already heard about Skeates's arrival from a passing neighbor. Skeates was bringing most of his own staff and would only be filling in gaps here and there with former Munro workers.

Over supper, they could not avoid what was on everyone's minds.

Rory set down his fork. "I cannae stomach the thought of that cheat in our home."

The captain looked from Rory to Angus. "Cheat?"

Angus cast a sharp eye toward Rory. "We've no proof."

Rory looked at his father. "Angus feels certain the man cheated. The game was too coincidental to be anything else."

"But," Angus said firmly, "we'll not share our suspicions. We've been brought low enough. Casting aspersions on Skeates's character just makes us look worse."

"Aye." The captain leaned back, deep in thought.

"I cannae say where I heard it, but I'm told Mr. Skeates is a terrible man to the folk who work downstairs," Effie said.

Lucy leaned forward, her eyes bright with interest. "Terrible? How so?"

Effie lowered her eyes. "He takes liberties. Unwanted liberties." She glanced toward Angus, which did not go unnoticed by him.

His temper flared. "That is not what I did, and you ken it."

Effie stood, looking shocked. "I didnae say that you did! Now look, Mr. Angus Munro, you can talk how you like when I'm in your house, but now you're in mine." She went to her box bed and sat on the edge with her arms folded.

Lucy quietly said, "Angus, I think she only looked at you to distinguish between you and Skeates. No one's accusing you of anything."

His eyes were ablaze. "I would never force myself on a woman. Why would I have to?"

"Go talk to her," Lucy whispered.

Angus sat down beside Effie, and they quietly talked.

Lucy looked over at the pair. Angus had the sort of dangerous good looks that a naïve girl could fall prey to and had in this case. She wondered how Effie could still be so kind to him when he had so cruelly rejected her. Effie must still harbor feelings, which saddened Lucy.

The only way Lucy could find Angus palatable was to accept him as the person he was even though he was far from the man he could have been. And yet he had changed since she'd known him. A month ago, she would never have imagined him working about the croft as he did, not complaining when painful blisters and calluses formed on his hands. In truth, he never complained. She had to respect him for that.

The captain stared at the fire with narrowing eyes. "That Skeates is a scoundrel, no doubt about that. What else do we know about him?"

"The baron introduced him as his dear friend from the Lowlands who had recently arrived for a visit," Angus said.

The captain tapped his fingertips on the arm of his chair. "His dear friend whom no one had seen nor heard of before."

Angus looked at his father. "At the time, I had other things on my mind, but looking back, there was something not quite right about those two. The baron seemed, well, the best way I can describe it is uneasy. One didn't sense the sort of ease found between friends."

Rory leaned forward. "Just what are you suggesting?"

Angus shrugged. "Only that it was curious. As clouded as my good sense might have been, losing as I was, it struck me."

The captain studied Angus. "I wish we knew more about the dear friend Mr. Skeates."

"I can ask around." All eyes turned to Effie, whose eyes widened at seeing the captain's masked disbelief. "You do ken servants talk, do you not? I'll see what I can find out in the village tomorrow."

Lucy was making the beds up with clean linens while Rory puttered about. Suddenly, two arms circled her waist.

"Rory!" she cried out. "Don't scare me like that!"

Sporting that grin that she could not resist, he asked, "How would you like me to scare you?"

"Not at all, preferably."

He was instantly serious. "I see. If you dinnae like surprises, then I'll have to find someone else to share this lunch basket I've made." He shook his head, wincing.

She looked at him with a glint in her eye. "Well, I don't have anything against lunch."

"That's good, lass." He started toward the door, basket in hand. "After all, you'll need to keep up your strength for all that hard work you're doing." He opened the door.

She folded her arms and stared as he hesitated then walked through the door. An instant after the door closed, he stuck his head back inside. Lucy still stood, feet planted, with a broad smile on her face.

Having had his bluff called, Rory tilted his head toward the outdoors. "Well, all right then, come on."

Lucy laughed as she untied her apron and rushed out to join him.

It was a vigorous uphill hike, but they were rewarded with a view that took Lucy's breath away. "It never looks quite the same, does it?"

His eyes locked on hers. "No. One time's more beautiful than the next."

"So you think flattery will win me over?" She didn't tell him that the soft look in his eyes was enough.

"I was hoping." He smiled, but it faded, replaced by a deeper emotion.

The wind swept over the top of the mountain. Lucy shivered and stretched out a quilt to sit on. She pulled a second quilt about her shoulders and offered to share half with Rory. "You realize it's November. Not quite picnic weather."

"Aye, but..." He sighed. "I'm going daft from the sight of you day after day."

"I get that a lot, although not in a good way."

He laughed and swept her into his embrace. "No man could love you as I do."

"Rory—" She was going to tell him she loved him, but her lips found his, and any words in her mind fled. All she knew was the feel of her hands on his shoulders and chest and the warmth of his body against hers. The strength of the passion that fueled his embrace and his touch drove her longing. She reveled in the weight of his body on hers. It no longer mattered to her where they were, whether they were in her time or his, as long as they were together. They had this moment, which Rory had stolen, alone at the top of the hill.

RORY BROUGHT in some peat for the fire, while Lucy began fixing a stew with the rabbit Angus had caught for dinner. When she'd first set eyes upon it, she'd had to turn away. Seeing her reaction, Rory had come to her rescue as Angus stood wondering what was the matter. "Dinnae fash, lass, we'll have this gutted and skinned in no time."

"Don't! I don't want to know what you're doing or how. I'm just going to pretend it came out of a shrink-wrapped package from the grocery store." She didn't care if no one had any idea what she was talking about. She'd done pretty darn well at adjusting to life in 1746, but there were some things she might never grow used to.

Luckily for her, Effie arrived home in time to complete the dead-animal portion of the evening's culinary festivities.

As they sat down for their meal, Angus offered to say grace. Effie looked shocked, while Lucy just looked. If she didn't know him better, she would say Angus was changing, and for the better. She glanced at Rory, but he was too fully absorbed in his meal to take notice.

"I had a chat in the village with Annie, the scullery maid at the castle," Effie said. "Well, now she's been taken on by the Baron of Swordale—as a housemaid, no less. I'd never have thought it, but she seems to be getting on well enough."

Lucy thought she detected a subtle rivalry there, but given the circumstances, who could blame the girl?

Effie continued. "Well, I was asking about Mr. Skeates, and she said that same gentleman happened to call on the baron this past week. She happened to be outside His Lordship's drawing room when she heard loud voices. Mr. Skeates—for she knew it was not His Lordship's voice—well, he was ordering the baron about in no uncertain terms."

"Skeates was ordering Swordale? In his own home?" the captain asked, appalled.

"About what?" Rory asked. "What were his exact words?"

Effie sighed. "I tried to get it out of her, but she couldnae remember. All she could say was that the two men had words, and when Mr. Skeates paused at the door to put on his hat, he looked very pleased with himself."

"Did he?" Angus asked, intrigued.

"Aye, but His Lordship was not. As soon as Mr. Skeates was gone, he called for the butler."

Wendy's eyes twinkled. "Your friend didn't miss much, did she?"

"No, she never has." Effie raised her eyebrows and smiled. "Shortly after, they were told to prepare for a large party. It's to be a week from Saturday."

Rory leaned back, brow furrowed. "Hmm... it would seem our Mr. Skeates has called for a party at the baron's expense."

Angus scowled. "But why would he not host his own party? He's certainly won enough funds to entertain the whole of the Highlands in style."

"Unless he needs introduction to Swordale's friends," Rory said.

The captain turned to Angus. "What sort of man would you judge Mr. Skeates to be just from looking at him?"

"Rather coarse," Angus said without hesitation.

The captain nodded. "And friends? Only those he has met through his so-called 'dear friend' Swordale?"

Rory studied his father. "Skeates has something on Swordale?"

The captain gave a knowing nod. "And..."

Rory's eyes brightened. "Either he's blackmailing him, or the baron owes him, and this is payment for a debt."

Angus's eyes darkened. "We need to go to this party."

Rory eyed Angus and shook his head slowly. "Do you think that's a good idea right now?"

Angus bristled. "I'll not gamble if that's what you're thinking. I want to observe."

"Observe what?" Rory asked, still doubting his brother.

"I want to observe them together. What if Skeates has

set up a scheme using Swordale's friends as his marks? If he has, Swordale knows it, but Skeates has something on him, so he's forced to comply. Skeates is good, or I would have seen something already. But everyone makes mistakes, and he's due for one."

"You're just guessing," Rory said.

"Aye. You can say what you want about how I've lived my life, but I've a bit of experience to back up my guess."

Rory reluctantly agreed but then shook his head.

Angus's eyes shone. "There's only one way to be sure."

Rory's jaw tightened. "Oh no. We dinnae need to be sure. What we need is to live our lives without risking what little we have left."

Angus was losing his patience. "And it is precious little. Do you want to live like this forever? How long do you think it will be before the new laird takes stock of his holdings and forces us out of this croft to make way for new tenants?"

Effie took in a sharp breath.

Lucy leaned toward Rory. "Is this true? Could he send us away?"

Rory tore his glare from Angus. "Aye. Effie doesnae own this croft. I suppose it's possible he'll not ken how to run an estate of this size. It could take weeks before he gets around to looking into the rent from his crofters or sends us all on our way."

Lucy put her hand on Rory's. "Then we have to do something."

Angus watched the exchange with the thrill of a win in his eyes.

Rory rose from his chair to go look out the window, arms folded.

The captain spoke in measured tones. "If he's a cheat, and we're able to expose him, we could reclaim our fortune."

Lost in thoughts that put a gleam in his eyes, Angus leaned back and looked at the beams overhead, while across the room, Rory turned to his father with a questioning look. The captain answered with a nod.

Rory went over and sat beside Lucy.

"Rory, how can you pass up a chance to get your home back?" She looked into his eyes with confidence in the effort if not the outcome. When he remained reluctant, she said, "The estate has been in your family for generations. You at least need to try."

He grasped her hand and turned to his father. "This could turn out badly."

His father nodded but shrugged.

"Or not," Lucy said.

Effie watched, her eyes lit with the excitement of a new adventure.

CHAPTER 17
THE PLAN

Angus pulled out his cards and faro board and proceeded to spend the next afternoon tutoring Lucy and Wendy on the card game of faro. They hoped simply to watch, but they needed to know how to play if they were to detect any cheating. Every moment spent practicing would make them readier.

Having voiced some concerns, the captain put on his best clothes and went calling on an old friend. Rory was off to the inn to gather what information he could about Skeates. Meanwhile, Effie disappeared on errands unknown.

The late-afternoon November sun made its early descent to the hilly horizon as Rory was first to return. He closed the door and bumped into a table on his way across the room.

Angus looked up. "I dinnae ken what you've learned, but your mood's looking better."

Rory's grin prompted Angus to laugh. "Good God, man, you're sottered!"

Lucy furrowed her brow. "Sottered?"

Angus's eyes sparkled with glee. "Your lad's drunk."

Rory plopped down on a chair and nearly lost his balance in the process. "Aye, well, I had a wee dram or two as I listened to some interesting stories—well, one story, really, but one repeated across Easter Ross."

"Skeates." Lucy handed the card deck to Angus, who finished packing up the faro board.

Rory's mouth turned up at the corner. "Aye."

Lucy smiled. "Easy there, laddie." When he looked at her with a furrowed brow, she added proudly, "How's my accent?"

He grasped her hand and looked up with the most adorably boyish smile she'd ever seen. "Dinnae change for me, bonnie Lucy. I love you too much."

Lucy caught an amused look from her mother just before Rory pulled her onto his lap and circled his arms about her waist.

"Effie must have some coffee around here." Wendy suppressed her amusement as she settled for tea and put the kettle over the fire.

As Rory nuzzled his way down Lucy's neck, she caught Angus grinning and gently extricated herself from Rory's embrace, stepping away as he reached out. "Rory. Why don't you tell us all about Mr. Skeates?"

He grinned then grew somber. "You ken I'd do anything for you." His eyes moistened.

Astonished, Lucy nodded then glanced with wonder at Angus.

He shrugged. "I've never seen him like this."

Rory heard him and said, "Everyone feels terrible

about what happened. They all insisted on buying me drinks. I couldnae disappoint them."

"Oh, I doubt anyone's been disappointed." Lucy combed her fingers through Rory's hair as he drifted off for a nap by the fire.

In a half hour's time, Rory awoke and had sobered enough to regale them with stories of Mr. Skeates's exploits. By then, the captain had returned, having secured an invitation to the upcoming party.

From what Rory had gathered from his friends at the inn, a dozen or so people in Easter Ross shared similar suspicions about Mr. Skeates, although no one had lost as much as the Munros had. Still, too many had lost, and it had happened too neatly. A tide of displeasure was rising. Few people thought Skeates would last long in these parts. Although Swordale had vouched for the man, ensuring that any doubts would remain unvoiced out of deference to him, fewer and fewer were sitting down at his gaming table. Rory imagined Skeates would sense the tide turning before long and move on to other fishing grounds. If they were right about the man, that was a pattern he'd repeated countless times before coming there.

Effie returned after dark.

"We were worried about you," Wendy said before anyone else could voice like concerns.

Effie set down her creel of peat. She unloaded the top layer of bricks to reveal crumpled silk.

"My gown!"

Effie smiled and pulled out Lucy's best gown and the undergarments that went with it.

"And my slippers! But how did you get this?"

"My friend Annie, who works as a chambermaid there, has been sneaking our clothing down the servants' stairway to Mrs. MacEddie. I'll be stopping by to visit Mrs. MacEddie on my way back from the peat bogs for the next few days. If anyone asks, she'll tell them I've been trying to peddle my peat to the castle. They'll pity me but think nothing more of it."

Angus's eyes shone. "Effie, you're a wonder!"

Her eyes flickered toward him, but she turned and put her creel in the corner. "In a few trips, I should have all the clothes that you'll need for your party."

Rory's expression darkened. "Effie, you cannae do this."

"But I already have, and I will do it again until I've finished."

"Effie." Angus stared as though he'd never really seen her.

For the first time since Lucy had known him, Angus was speechless.

But Rory was not. "Do you ken if you're caught, you'll be thrown into jail and tried as a common thief? You'd be transported. It's too risky. I cannae allow it."

Effie stopped her supper preparations. "Rory, I thank you for your concern, but I'm no longer your responsibility. I dinnae need your permission." Effie turned and went on with her cooking, while the Munro men offered no further protest.

At some point, the balance had shifted among them. They were six people on equal footing, all working together. Some wanted to reclaim old lives, while others wished to build new ones. But regardless of wishes or wants or of how the current situation turned out, they would not be the same.

ON THE NIGHT of the party, they were all dressed and ready to go. Effie had spent the day pressing their clothing and fixing Wendy's and Lucy's hair. Effie was too well known as a maid in the area to risk posing as a guest with the others, so she stayed behind. They didn't have access to a proper carriage, so they borrowed a wagon and horses to take them to the baron's estate. The plan was to leave the horses and wagon tethered to a tree out of sight then walk over the hill to the home. If need be, they would offer an excuse about a broken wheel or lame horse.

By the time they arrived, a thin coating of snow covered the ground. Lucy wore patens to protect her fragile silk shoes during the walk to the house, but she and her mother still had to take great pains to lift their skirts and keep them from getting wet or soiled. They managed to make it inside looking as though they'd stepped down from a carriage outside of the door. With smiles and sighs of relief, they were ready to take on the evening.

There'd been a good deal of discussion over the accents. Since neither Lucy nor Wendy knew when the American accent had developed, they took a chance that being from foreign soil would be enough to explain away their unusual speech. To be safe, they planned to leave as much talk as possible to the men. While Wendy saw it as sort of a game, Lucy thought it might be the most challenging part of the evening. But there they were, and she was determined to make the evening the success that it desperately needed to be.

"Miss Buchanan, you look lovely," Rory said with an admiring smile.

She thanked him as she looked about the room. Perhaps two dozen guests stood about, talking. Her pulse raced.

He leaned closer and slipped his hand in hers. "I'm right here."

Lucy took a deep breath and exhaled. "Okay. Here we go." She looked over to find her mother on the captain's arm, looking as if she'd spent her whole life rubbing elbows with nobles.

After a blur of introductions, they made their way to a room with a wall of tall windows covered with pale-blue silk brocade curtains and velvet-upholstered chairs. A table was set up in the corner with a faro board and cards. A small group was quietly playing. Rory cast a knowing look at Angus, who appeared poised and ready. Angus had sworn off gambling, and they lacked money with which to gamble, anyway. While the captain had produced a secret stash of bank notes and jewels, they'd all agreed it could only be used as a last resort.

They set about observing the card play. Although Angus insisted he would be all right, Lucy had never felt comfortable bringing him there. But he knew far more than any of them about the game, which would make him the most likely to detect any irregularities. So despite this being the last place Angus needed to be, they took a chance for the sake of the cause. Even without playing, theirs were the highest stakes in the room.

Throughout the evening, a number of guests surreptitiously offered the Munro men words of support and encouraging nods. Angus may have had his problems, but the family was highly respected in spite of their spectacular loss of financial standing. A handful of people had begged off of the game and stood watching. They confided to Rory that Mr. Skeates had taken enough from their pockets over the past several weeks that they would rather give someone else a turn to lose. There were murmurs that Lucy couldn't hear, but from the way people eyed Skeates, it wasn't a far leap to conclude there were others who shared their suspicions.

The Munro party spread out and positioned themselves in strategic locations about the table so they were poised to see from all angles. While Angus had taught them the rudiments of the game, there were so many nuances Lucy hadn't been able to grasp in the short time they'd had. And this game moved much faster than their practice game in the croft. In addition to the speed of play, Angus hadn't told them how quietly engrossed all the players would be. The air was electric. She supposed she would have been as intensely involved in a game that could cost her everything she owned in the world.

As one hour then another wore on, Lucy grew weary and had to work harder to maintain concentration. After all of their trouble, perhaps Skeates was simply too good for her to notice him cheating. Or maybe he wasn't cheating at all. Maybe Angus had simply suffered a string of bad luck.

Then it happened. Skeates drew the queen of diamonds. Hadn't she seen the same card at play earlier in the game? She looked at Rory then at each of the others, but no one seemed bothered. Baron Campbell was acting as casekeeper, charged with adjusting an abacus-like device to keep track of the cards as they were drawn. He was only then moving a disc to show that the queen of diamonds card had been played. Had Lucy been recalling that card from a previous round?

She wanted to discuss it with Angus, or even Rory. He'd played faro before. But it was as quiet as a church in the room, and she didn't want to risk drawing anyone's notice. As the next round began, she kept a sharp eye on the cards and the casekeeper, trying to keep track of the cards that were played. It wasn't a perfect system, but it was the best she could do.

As the last ace was drawn, the baron moved the marker as was proper, but three turns later, she noticed it had been moved back. If a dealer and casekeeper worked together, it wouldn't be that difficult to get away with cheating. Yet no one else seemed aware of the discrepancy. Was she the one in error? She waited and watched. If another ace appeared, she would have proof. But one had not appeared.

They were nearly at the end of the deck when one of the players asked if this would be the last card before Skeates called the turn. Thanks to Angus's teaching, she remembered that the final round was played with the final three cards of the deck.

Skeates turned over the next card. There it was—a fifth ace. Lucy watched the casekeeper move the marker for the aces, which he'd already done in this round. She looked at Rory, Angus, and the others. But with no confirmation from them, she had to rely upon her recollection. If she called him on it, she risked having him hide the extra card, leaving her looking foolish and, worse, missing what might be their best chance to expose Skeates. There was no time to think.

Either way, she was going to look foolish. She started

to stand but pretended to lose her balance. She fell, grabbing the table where the stack of cards lay, and she took the deck down with her. All that remained were the last three cards on the table, which were visible to all.

"Oh, I'm so sorry." As she rose, she knocked a drink onto Skeates's lap. As he sprang to his feet and looked down at the spill, Lucy handed the deck over to Angus. "Oh, look what I've done! Mr. Munro, would you mind counting these cards, please? I'd hate to think that I'd lost one when I fell."

Angus gave her a questioning look, which she met with her most direct stare. Next, she discovered why men used to help ladies so much. As she tried to rise, she kept stepping on the voluminous folds of her skirts. If it weren't for Rory, she might never have made it to her feet. At least that portion of her histrionics was believable.

Once on her feet, Lucy joined a curious audience of over a dozen players and onlookers as Angus counted. "Forty-seven, forty-eight, forty-nine, fifty cards." Angus looked first at Skeates then at the baron. "And we all ken there are three on the table."

"Fifty-three cards." Rory eyed Skeates. "Isn't that one too many?"

Skeates had no place to go. They'd set up the game in a corner, presumably to conceal their actions on the dealer's side of the table. But now Skeates was trapped in his own scheme.

"Lord Campbell, may we be civilized about this?" the captain asked.

"You have my word," the baron answered.

Skeates made a run for it, but the numerous people he'd swindled were happy to catch and restrain him.

After Skeates was secured, the baron said, "I owed him too much. He forced me to assist him, or he'd have taken all this from me. I never wanted to do it."

"We'll sort it all out in court," the captain said.

Rory eyed Skeates for a moment then turned to the baron. "My lord, do you have anyplace we can hold him until we can send for the proper authorities?"

The baron's eyes brightened. "It's never used anymore, but we do have a dungeon."

"Allow me," Angus said, gripping Skeates's arm. Rory grabbed hold of the other, and they escorted Mr. Skeates to the baronial dungeon.

CHAPTER 18
THE UNEXPECTED

The night sky was black with a sprinkling of stars when the wagon pulled up to the croft. Lucy threw open the door and rushed inside to Effie.

"We did it, Effie! We caught Skeates!" She hugged Effie then squeezed both of the girl's hands.

"Well, that's grand!" Effie stroked the small mound on her belly. Would you like some tea?"

"I'll make it," Angus said.

Lucy tried not to look stunned. She plopped onto a chair beside Effie.

"It was Lucy who did it," Rory chimed from the doorway.

Lucy shook her head modestly. "Effie made it all happen. We'd have had nothing proper to wear, or a roof over our heads, without you."

Effie smoothed her skirt over her knees. "Anyone would have done the same."

Angus leaned against the wall, arms folded, smiling at Effie. "Except no one offered but you."

Effie's fleeting smile came and went.

"There's the water," Angus said. He brought Effie a cup of tea and sat on the edge of the box bed.

Rory made his way to Lucy's chair and stood behind it. She leaned into his hand as his fingers swept over her cheek, then his hands came to rest on her shoulders. She leaned back with a satisfied sigh and caught sight of the captain and Wendy engaged in a quiet tête-à-tête on the edge of the second box bed. It wasn't so much that they were sitting on the bed that caught Lucy's attention. The croft was small, with little furniture, so everyone used the beds like sofas. What she noticed was the hushed, personal way they were talking.

As she pondered the captain and her mother, Angus swept her up into a dance as he sang.

"Careful!" she said as he swung her around. "This skirt could take out half the furniture and the peat fire as well."

"Sorry, madam. I was overwhelmed by your splendor and keen eye at the gaming tables."

Seeing Effie turn sharply, Angus quietly told her, "I didnae play."

Effie picked up her knitting. "'Tis none of my business if you did."

"May I?" Rory asked Angus then took Lucy's hand and led her away from the fire and the furniture, to the side of the room. He held out his hand, slipped the other about her waist, and began slowly to dance.

"There's no music," she whispered.

"You are my music."

"Oh, that, Mr. Rory Munro, is a line." His admiring stare made her weak in the knees, but she hid it.

"A line?"

"Something you say to charm all the ladies."

He looked a little surprised. "You're the only one I want to charm." That gentle, unaffected manner of his was certainly working. She leaned into his arm, and their dance slowed to an embrace. He leaned close to her ear. "Thank you."

She looked up, ready to offer a modest reply, but seeing his unguarded expression, she said, "I just want you to have everything you deserve."

"I dinnae deserve you."

"Well, you've got me."

He tightened his arms about her and whispered, "And I'd have you right now if we were alone."

FINLAY SKEATES STOOD before a bailie in the Inverness Police Court. The Munro family was present, along with Lucy, Wendy, and Effie. Since the pivotal game in which Angus had lost everything, a number of subsequent victims had suffered varying degrees of losses, so they were all present.

Lucy was surprised to learn that, in Scotland, eighteenth-century defendants rarely retained legal counsel, and Skeates was no exception.

"You are charged with cheating at cards," the magistrate said. "Is that right?"

"I can't help it if people don't like to lose to a superior player."

"Superior?"

"Aye."

The magistrate smiled. "It says here that you've been on quite a winning streak."

Skeates shrugged.

"Is there anyone present who has fallen victim to Mr. Skeates and his superior card-playing skills?"

Angus and more than a dozen others stood.

The magistrate pored over the papers in his hands. "Who among you can offer proof of the cheating?"

"I can, your honor," Lucy said.

He jerked his head toward her. "Who's responsible for this woman?"

Lucy leaned forward. "Responsible? I am."

"I am." Rory cast a stern look at her, which only irritated her more.

The magistrate narrowed his eyes. "Silence her, would you?"

Lucy's mouth opened, but Rory lowered his voice and spoke through a frustrated smile. "Do you want us to lose?"

She was too stunned to react.

Angus leaned over. "The court doesn't recognize women," he whispered.

How long her jaw hung open, Lucy couldn't have been sure. It was probably somewhere around the same amount of time it took her to mentally list the things she did not like about the eighteenth century. While she would have preferred to make an issue of her right to speak for herself, she could not disagree that the more pressing concern at the moment was getting the Munro estate back in their possession. And so she behaved. But the court couldn't force her to like it.

Rory finished testifying about the fifty-third card, and

several witnesses confirmed his accounting. Twenty minutes after the proceeding had begun, it was over, and they had their property back.

Baron Campbell was found to have operated under duress and was sentenced to one week in jail, which he had already served. Skeates would serve six months for his crime.

As they all walked out, overjoyed and relieved, Lucy muttered to her mother, "Wow, that was quick. Cutting out all the lawyers and women is a real time-saver."

Wendy's eyes sparkled. "Well, you wanted eighteenth century; you got eighteenth century."

Lucy tilted her head toward Rory. "No, I just wanted him."

THE SERVANTS all gathered in front of the castle to greet them upon their return. The butler welcomed the captain back home with dignified words and warmth in his eyes. Captain Munro paused inside the doorway to take in the sight of the entrance call, the grand stairway, and the hallway that led to his library. As the rest of them followed and turned to head for the library, Effie veered off toward the kitchen, but Angus clasped her hand to stop her.

"Effie, come join us."

"We're back, Mr. Munro." She lowered her eyes, discreetly slipped her hand from his, and walked away.

Angus pensively watched the door close behind Effie.

Lucy took a step toward him, but Rory touched her arm. "Leave him be, lass."

Reluctantly, Lucy left Angus behind and joined Rory. "I can't help but feel sorry for him."

Rory smiled to himself. "Aye, well, that's what he does. He knocks everything down then feels sorry when the pieces fall on him." He took a deep breath and lowered his voice. "But this time, the pieces fell on all of us."

Lucy slipped her arm into Rory's. "But we're back now. Let's move forward."

"Tell that to Effie." In Rory's dark eyes, Lucy saw how the pain of his past stood in the way of his future. When he looked at Effie, he seemed to see Margery all over again. But beyond that, at the root of all things painful, was Angus.

Along came Lucy feeling sorry for Angus. Perhaps his ability to elicit that response was not only Angus's saving grace, but also his curse. He had recovered and moved on to repeat his mistakes, and because of his boyish charm, those around him had always forgiven him. Except Rory. Lucy couldn't fault him for that, but she feared this dark cloud of a family dynamic would cast its shadow over her relationship with Rory for more years to come.

As they walked into the library, Captain Munro poured champagne into glasses. He stopped and looked up. "Where's Effie?"

"She's gone to the kitchen," Angus said. "I dinnae think she felt comfortable in here with us. With me."

The captain frowned and looked down, swallowing back his emotions. "Would someone go— No, I'll go fetch her."

The glimmer in Angus's eyes darkened. He finished his champagne, poured a whisky, and went to the window.

Lucy's mother had gone with the captain to find Effie, leaving Angus by the window, brooding, and Rory at the fire beside Lucy.

She studied Angus. "He's got to have learned something from this."

"Don't expect too much. You'll just be disappointed."

She chose not to respond. It was neither the time nor the place.

"I'm sorry," Rory said. "But I've been through this too many times."

With a nod, Lucy looked over at Angus, who couldn't have looked more miserable.

Rory turned his gaze on Lucy. His dark eyes never ceased to affect her. "Do you not see that his actions affect us and our future? I'll not tether you to a life of financial uncertainty."

In hushed protest, she said, "It's not your wealth that I fell in love with. It's you. Whether here, in a croft, in my mother's small house—no matter what happens or where we might find ourselves, I'll love you."

He made a weak effort at a smile and pulled her into his arms. "And I love you too much to subject you to Angus's whims."

She could not ignore the twinge of uneasiness his words prompted. "What are you saying?"

Captain Munro and Wendy returned with Effie in tow, and she looked shyly appreciative.

The captain cleared his throat. "This young lady is no longer in our employ. She did this family a tremendous service at a time when others turned away in discomfort over being so close to such failure—as if they might catch it."

Angus flinched.

Captain Munro continued. "But Effie stood by us. She gave us a home, and she smuggled our clothes out so we could go expose Skeates as a card cheat and thief. Now it is our turn to stand by her and return the favor. After all we've been through, I cannae imagine her not being part of our household—not as a servant, but as part of our family. This will be her home and the home of her child, my grandchild, for as long as they live."

Effie's eyes welled with tears. She turned her head slowly back and forth as though she might protest if she weren't so stunned by the offer.

Lucy looked at the others, who were all smiling. Except Angus. If Lucy didn't know better, she might have thought that hopeless, lost look in his eyes, as they lingered on Effie, revealed tender feelings.

The captain held up his glass. "To Effie and to coming home." The captain's own eyes looked a bit misty as he put on a bright face. "Now then, this is a celebration!" He opened another bottle of champagne, and serious thoughts gave way to joy and laughter.

FOLLOWING SUPPER, Effie and the captain settled a matter that had troubled her since his invitation. Reluctant to leave her at her home, he convinced her to stay at least until after the baby was born. After that, they would talk more about it. He made a convincing enough case that she finally agreed.

As the captain's attention was drawn elsewhere,

Angus appeared before her. "I must speak with you, Effie."

Effie shook her head, but Angus touched her arm. "Please?"

He led her to a far corner of the library. She looked about, wishing she could escape.

Angus folded and unfolded his arms and let them hang loosely. "I've made some mistakes." Her eyes widened, and her lips parted. Before she could speak, he hastened to say, "Terrible ones. And I ken that I've hurt you."

Her brow furrowed as she tamped down the pain he'd brought rushing back.

"I'm not the same man I was when—"

"Angus." She shook her head and looked anywhere but at him.

"Effie, I ken I was terrible to you, and I... if I could go back, I would never have hurt you like that."

She managed to look at him. "I thank you for your apology. I do. And I accept it. But if I'm to stay here 'til the bairn is born, we cannae speak of it again." She didn't tell him that was because it was too painful or that he'd broken her heart.

"Marry me, Effie."

Her heart stopped.

He took her hands in his. "Please. I—I think I must have been blinded by the difference in our stations in life. I didn't want to believe I could love you. But God help me, I do. Will you marry me?"

How many times had she dreamed this moment? She'd let herself love him before she had known what love was or the power of its grip on her heart.

The look in his eyes tugged at her heart. Even now he could sway her to feel something for him. He was all dark eyes, winning grin, and unbridled energy. But boyish charm was no longer enough. She would marry a man or not marry at all.

"No. I'm sorry." She fled the library and rushed up to her room.

CHAPTER 19
THE ANNOUNCEMENT

Wendy found Lucy in the seldom-used gallery with cushioned window seats at each window that looked out over the frost-coated Highlands. "This is one of my favorite spots. Mind if I join you?"

"Not at all." Lucy patted the bench cushion.

"It's amazing here, isn't it?"

Lucy nodded. Her mother looked as happy as she sounded. "So it's worked out okay for you?"

Wendy gave her a look as if she were crazy for asking.

"You came here for me; you gave up so much," Lucy explained.

Wendy smiled and waved at the air. "Shh! No more worries."

"Sure?"

"Positive." Wendy leaned back and looked at the view. "And what about you?"

"Me?"

"And Rory..."

Startled, Lucy asked, "Why? Do you know something?"

An amused smile teased Wendy's face. "I do now."

Lucy rolled her eyes. "Which is why I will never play poker."

Wendy couldn't help but chuckle. "Good call."

With a sigh, Lucy leaned her head back against the wall. "He's not happy. I love him so much that it aches to see him like this." She turned and looked helplessly at her mother. "What can I do?"

"Nothing. That's the hardest thing about love. You can't make everything better."

"Wrong answer."

"Right question, though. What you do is love him. Be there."

"I am, but he won't talk about it."

Wendy put her hand on Lucy's. "When he's ready, you'll be there."

"How do you know that he'll ever be ready?"

"Because I've been there—on the talking and listening sides. Everyone needs that at some point."

Lucy exhaled, discouraged. "In a way, it was easier back at the croft. Life was simple. We got up. We did the chores that we had to for food, warmth, and shelter. And we went to bed, exhausted. Rinse and repeat."

Wendy lifted an eyebrow. "Life isn't so horrible, is it? You're living in a castle. Not much to complain about there."

"That's just it. It is wonderful, but it's all Angus's. And Rory can't like that. We're all back here for now, but what if it happens again?"

"You think that's what's bothering Rory?"

"Why wouldn't it? Rory sweated bullets to keep this place thriving, and then, in one fell swoop, Angus destroyed it."

"I'm sure he never meant to hurt anyone."

Lucy rolled her eyes in frustration. "Of course not. But he did it. Like a child, he saw only the moment. And because of his guileless charm, we forgave him—as if he were a child. Meanwhile, Rory's an adult with no power to protect his own family and home."

Footsteps sounded along the wooden floor outside of the gallery. The two women stared, wide-eyed, and Lucy rushed to the door in time to catch a glimpse of plaid flutter and disappear around the corner.

RORY EXCUSED himself from the breakfast table. "I'm going for a ride."

Lucy watched him walk out the door then looked at her mother and Captain Munro. There was nothing to say. Angus had disappeared three days ago with no warning and no explanation. Since then, Rory had barely spoken to anyone. No one had said anything, but they all had to be thinking the same thing. Angus had gone off on a gambling bender.

When she could no longer hold back, Lucy turned to the captain. "Has Angus ever been gone this long?"

"No." His answer was quiet and quick.

In silence, they finished their breakfast and went their separate ways. Lucy set down the book she'd been staring at without being able to read, then she donned an arisaid and went out to the garden. Despite having nowhere in particular to go, she walked briskly. Was it frustration or anger? She wasn't sure what she felt. She only knew that she'd lost control of her life. Since she'd first walked through the stone chamber, she'd lost any sense of where her life was going.

No, in truth it had happened before that, at the moment Tyler had called off the wedding. Until then, she'd known exactly what her life was and what it would be. It had all been well ordered and secure. But then Tyler had done what he did, and she'd run. If only she'd left and gone home. One of them would have moved out, but then her life would have settled back into a rhythm—alone but secure. She would have still had her job, her friends, and her way of life.

But she *had* run. It was she who had made that decision, and she who had fallen in love. Now she had to face the truth nobody had told her about: love was hard.

"Lucy."

She didn't have to turn to know it was Rory, but she did.

He was striding toward her. "We need to talk."

Nothing good ever followed those words. "Okay."

He touched her cheek. "You're so cold. Let's go inside by the fire."

She nodded and took the arm he offered. She asked him about his ride, and they spoke of the weather as if their lives at the castle didn't hang in the balance.

At the door to the library, he paused. "I've asked my father and your mother to join us."

Lucy didn't ask why. She wasn't sure she wanted to know. Yet when she stepped through the doorway, she would have no choice.

Once all four were seated, Rory wasted no time. "These past three days, I doubt any of us have been able to get the same thought from our minds."

The captain's eyes were dark and distant, while Wendy displayed more generous concern.

Rory glanced at Lucy, then his eyes settled upon his father. "First, I wish to make it clear that I respect your decision regarding this estate. It's not unusual for a father to deed his estate to his firstborn son. Regardless of whether you could've foreseen what happened to us, happen it did. And now, with Angus having been gone these three days, it takes little imagination to surmise what has happened. While I'd hoped he would learn his lesson, I fear it's a situation over which he has no control.

"I have agonized these past three days, as well as the days, months, and years before that. As it affects all of us sitting here, I feel I must share with you what I'm thinking—or rather, what I'm planning. I've been unable to plan for my own life while I've been subject to Angus's weaknesses and excesses. I can no longer endure it. I must have my own life over which I have some control."

Lucy looked up, feeling suddenly excluded, but then his eyes settled on hers with the warmth that allayed any doubts. He looked down and smiled and then looked up at Wendy. "I am deeply in love with your daughter."

When he looked back at Lucy, she felt him gaze into her soul. "I have not felt the freedom that a home and financial security would afford. But if I am to ask this woman to share my life, then I must have a life I can offer."

Lucy felt as if her heart were in her throat.

"And so I feel I've no choice but to leave." He lifted

his eyes to look off in the distance, avoiding the shocked expressions that followed his announcement.

"Leave?" Lucy couldn't believe what she was hearing. She'd given up too much to be there, only to have him sacrifice what they had together because of some misguided notion of protecting her. Lucy stopped before saying more. She wanted to tell him no, that this was not what she had come there for or what she wanted. She'd come because her mother had practically dragged her, knowing how much Lucy loved Rory. But she'd wanted to come and be with him no matter what. He'd been willing to do that for her. Before they'd learned about Angus's gambling loss, Rory had never brought up the idea of coming back to his home in the past. He would have accepted his life in her time because he loved her that much. Surely, she owed him the same.

Rory smiled softly at her. "I ask you to think, truly think about what this would mean. There is land in a colony called South Carolina, where they're granting land at one hundred acres a man—fifty more for each person with him. Wendy, of course we would want you to join us, regardless. And Father, I ken you'd not want to leave your home, but if something were ever to go amiss, you would always be welcome."

Lucy's head spun. Leave Scotland for what was now a wilderness? When they arrived—*if* they arrived after a treacherous sea journey—they would have nothing but a large parcel of land. Then they would begin building from scratch—camping out, stripping logs, building a shelter, hunting and fishing for food. And if they survived that, they risked illness and attacks from Native Americans, whose land they would be taking. Lucy paused to consider that. It was one thing to look back at historical wrongs, but how could she participate in them with a full understanding of their ramifications?

Rory looked warmly at Lucy. "I ken that it's a grand scheme, but I want you to think upon it."

She could barely respond. "I love it here."

"So do I," Rory said calmly. "All I ask is that you think about it."

Lucy wanted to run back to the cairn or at least to someplace she could think. But that was always her knee-jerk response. This was something she had to face up to.

She looked at her mother. Of course, Wendy was bright-eyed. She obviously loved the idea.

Poor Captain Munro looked blindsided. "I think we could all use a wee dram."

"Yes," Wendy said as she got up to help pour and deliver the drinks.

Rory sat beside Lucy and lifted her hand to his lips. "I cannae go through it again—losing our home and watching what it put you through."

"What, scrubbing clothes and skinning animals for supper? How would life in the colonies be different from that?"

He leaned back in his chair. "It would be our land. We'd be building a life, not only for us, but for our children and their children."

Children? She hadn't even thought about children. And now he was talking about sailing to the colonies? As she imagined herself stripping the bark from the logs for their cabin, Wendy handed her a glass, which she threw back so fast that her mother could only blink slowly before she took the glass back for a refill. When Lucy had finished drink number two, she retired to the window seat to stare out at the magnificent Highlands.

It was beginning to snow. There was barely a dusting on the ground, but the mist nearly covered the tips of the mountains, making it hard to discern what was solid and real.

Rory sat down on the window seat, facing her, and looked out at the snow. "How many days have I spent like this, wondering what my brother was up to? But now that I ken how far he can go, all I think of is whether he's done it again. I'm daft to worry. 'Tis not even mine. I'm permitted to live here at Angus's pleasure, but I stand to lose what I think of as home for the same reason. A man cannae live like that, Lucy."

She turned from the window. "I love you. But at the moment, I can't say it's easy." She sighed sadly. "But I can't help myself now. I will go where you feel you must go because I've fallen in love and I have to be with you. The thing is, I've also fallen in love with this land. I feel like I've come home, and you're taking me from it."

"Again," he said, looking downward.

CHAPTER 20
HOME INDEED

Cradled in Rory's arms, Lucy sat and watched the sun set. Wendy and the captain murmured over a chessboard, and Effie had joined them, warming herself in a chair by the fire as she knitted. Since Rory's announcement, they'd all settled into quiet thought. Lucy began to think Rory was right to want to leave now with a memory of Kildermoor in its prime.

They heard someone open and close the front door. A moment later, Angus walked in and strode to the desk. "Good evening."

Rory lifted an eyebrow and muttered to Lucy, "He's got his winning face on, so we've someplace to sleep for the evening, at least."

"You've been gone for three days," Captain Munro said. "No one knew where you were."

"But we guessed," Rory said dryly.

Angus's mouth quirked at the corner. "I had some business to attend to."

Rory sneered. "Winning business, I hope."

Lucy cast a concerned glance at Rory. She couldn't blame him for feeling bitter, but she wondered what he had to gain by expressing it now.

"I said I'd not gamble, and I haven't." Angus handed some folded papers to his father. "I've just returned from our solicitor's office." He pointed to the papers. "Please read it."

Angus went to the mahogany desk and sat down while the captain read. The air was electric as the others watched with intense curiosity.

Captain Munro looked up at Angus. "You've deeded the property back to me?"

"To you 'and the heirs of your body,'" Angus recited.

The captain nodded in wonder as Rory asked, "In fee tail?"

Angus smiled at Rory. "Aye."

Lucy looked questioningly at Rory. "Fee tail? But what does that mean?"

Before Rory could answer, Angus said, "It means that Rory and I will inherit together, and not only will one of us not be able to sell or transfer the property without the other's approval, but our heirs will have an interest in it as well."

Rory slowly shook his head as he stared at Angus.

Angus looked at Effie. "And I've something for you." He pulled another paper from his coat pocket and handed it to her. "In short, this acknowledges the child you carry as my heir."

As her eyes filled with tears, she said, "Thank you. I'm sorry. I've been so emotional lately."

Angus looked tenderly at her then turned to the others. "I've never been very good at thinking of others, and I've managed to hurt everyone who's ever managed to care for me. I cannae change what I've done, but I can change the future. I can make sure no one in this family ever has to fear losing our home." His eyes flickered toward Rory and Lucy. "I've instructed the bank to deliver a modest annual sum to a separate account in my name. What remains is in your two names alone. I cannae touch it without your permission."

"Angus?" Looking as puzzled as he was pleased, the captain peered at his son.

With a satisfied smile, Angus said, "None of you will have to worry about your home or your future in it."

A moment of stunned silence was interrupted by the butler. "Excuse me, Effie—Miss Vass, rather—there's a Symon Culloch to see you."

"Symon?" Effie pushed up from her chair and excused herself as she followed the butler.

Seeing the blush in Effie's cheeks, Lucy smiled and leaned close to Rory. "That's her friend from the céilidh," she whispered.

Angus's eyes remained fixed upon Effie until she was gone from the room.

Interrupting whatever thoughts appeared to preoccupy Angus, Rory approached his brother and extended his hand. "Angus, I dinnae ken what to say. Thank you, of course. What you've done is too generous."

Angus gave Rory's shoulder a pat as he shook his head. "What I've done is the right thing. Now that it's done, there's no need to speak further of it." His eyes darkened as he looked into Rory's.

Rory nodded, and his eyes brightened. "Would you excuse me?"

Angus nodded.

Rory went to Lucy and dropped to one knee. She took in a sharp breath.

"Lucy Buchanan, I began falling in love the first moment I saw you, and I haven't stopped yet. Would you do me the honor of marrying me and of spending your life with me, here in our home?"

"Yes." It came out in a whisper. She blinked her moist eyes. "Yes!"

Rory leapt to his feet, swept her into his arms, and spun her around as his brother and their parents all clapped. Angus went to the door and called to the footman to bring some champagne from the cellar, then he returned to the joyous celebration. When the champagne and toasts were all done, Captain Munro turned to Wendy with a questioning look, and she nodded.

Captain Munro cleared his throat. "It appears we'll be having a double wedding."

Lucy and Rory both turned to Angus, but he shook his head, looking as confused as they were.

To Lucy's shock, the captain put his arm about Wendy's shoulders. "This lovely lady has done me the honor of agreeing to become my wife."

"What?" It came out louder than Lucy had meant. She apologized immediately and asked with more poise, "When did this happen?"

Captain Munro was a man of few words, but he looked at Wendy with glimmering eyes. "From the moment she moved into that croft, I found I could not take my eyes off her. And then when we talked, it was never enough. I began to look forward to having her in my days and in my life."

Wendy gazed into his eyes and turned back with a grin. "I just thought he was hot."

THE GREAT HALL of Kildermoor Castle was decked with holly and evergreens draped over the beams of the barrel-vault ceiling. The pine scent mingled with that of the roast goose and venison on the tables below. It was a magnificent feast, to which everyone within traveling distance had come. It was Saint Nicholas Day, but more importantly to all present, it was a grand wedding day.

A large Yule log blazed in the fireplace as the two couples were pronounced man and wife. Then the dancing began. First, a lone piper began, then the bodhrán joined in. Fiddle, pennywhistle, and singers came and went, depending upon how full their cups were.

Symon led Effie onto the floor, where she gingerly danced with her attentive partner. With a wistful smile, Angus watched.

As the next tune began, the parents traded partners with their newlywed children but were happy to trade back halfway into the song. Rory took Lucy's hand and smiled down at his wife. The truth was he'd barely stopped smiling since the celebration began. And Lucy, whose heart was so full that she thought it might burst, had traveled through time just to find her way home.

ACKNOWLEDGMENTS

Editing by Red Adept Editing
redadeptediting.com

THANK YOU!

Thank you for reading! If you enjoyed this book, please consider leaving a review or a rating on Amazon or your favorite bookstore. Your feedback helps other readers discover my work.

BOOK NEWS

Sign up for the J.L. Jarvis Journal for exclusive benefits, including free books, special offers, exclusive content, and updates on new releases: news.jljarvis.com

READING ORDER

Drake & Wilde Mysteries

#1 Love in the Time of Pumpkins

#2 Secrets in the Hollow

#3 Shadow of the Horseman

Standalones

A Kiss in the Rain

App-ily Ever After

Once Upon a Winter

The Red Rose

Highland Vow

Short Stories

Seasons of Love: A Short Story Collection

The Eleventh-Hour Pact

A Christmas Yarn

The Farmer and the Belle

Work-Crush Balance

Cedar Creek

(Can be read in any order)

Christmas at Cedar Creek

Snowstorm at Cedar Creek

Sunlight on Cedar Creek

Pine Harbor

(Reading Order)

#1 Allison's Pine Harbor Summer

#2 Evelyn's Pine Harbor Autumn

#3 Lydia's Pine Harbor Christmas

Holiday House

(Can be read in any order)

The Christmas Cabin

The Winter Lodge

The Lighthouse

The Christmas Castle

The Beach House

The Christmas Tree Inn

The Holiday Hideaway

Highland Passage

(Can be read in any order)

Highland Passage

Knight Errant

Lost Bride

Highland Soldiers

(Reading Order)

#1 The Enemy

#2 The Betrayal

#3 The Return

#4 The Wanderer

American Hearts

(Can be read in any order)

Secret Hearts

Forbidden Hearts

Runaway Hearts

For more information, visit jljarvis.com.

Get monthly book news at news.jljarvis.com.

ABOUT THE AUTHOR

J.L. Jarvis is a left-handed former opera singer/teacher/lawyer who writes books. She now lives and writes on a mountaintop in upstate New York.

jljarvis.com

facebook.com/jljarvis1writer

x.com/JLJarvis_writer

instagram.com/jljarvis.writer

bookbub.com/authors/j-l-jarvis

pinterest.com/jljarviswriter

goodreads.com/5106618.J_L_Jarvis

amazon.com/author/B005G0M2Z0

youtube.com/UC7kodjlaG-VcSZWhuYUUl_Q